Swe

"Forget I said ... ed
lightly. "You ... ...wn
without listeni... ...lems, too."

"Oh, but—"

"You shouldn't be such a good listener," he chided teasingly, tapping playfully on the tip of her nose, realizing, even as he did it, that the action must seem condescending.

Grace looked up at him with reproachful eyes, and he knew he had hurt her feelings. If she could only know that he was hurting himself more—that he would like nothing better than to pour his heart out to this hauntingly lovely young woman. Her lips were soft and pink, slightly parted, and he moved toward her as if drawn to a magnet.

Grace knew he was going to kiss her and she parted her lips further as she tilted her head toward his, seconds before his mouth claimed hers.

CAROLE MORTIMER, one of our most popular—and prolific—English authors, began writing in
the Harlequin Presents series in 1979. She now has
more than seventy bestselling romances to her credit
and shows no signs whatever of running out of plot
ideas. She writes strong traditional romances with a
distinctly modern appeal, and her winning way with
characters and romantic plot twists has earned her
an enthusiastic audience worldwide.

Books by Carole Mortimer

CAROLE MORTIMER

Saving Grace

Harlequin Books

TORONTO • NEW YORK • LONDON
AMSTERDAM • PARIS • SYDNEY • HAMBURG
STOCKHOLM • ATHENS • TOKYO • MILAN
MADRID • WARSAW • BUDAPEST • AUCKLAND

My husband, Frank,
All my love.

Harlequin Presents first edition April 1993
ISBN 0-373-11543-1

Original hardcover edition published in 1992
by Mills & Boon Limited

SAVING GRACE

PROLOGUE

'OUCH, Tim,' came the wounded cry. 'I told you not to do that!'

Silence followed the protest, and the man who had unwittingly stumbled upon the two hesitated among the undergrowth and bushes that shielded them from his view. And him from theirs.

Jordan had stopped his car and got out on to the roadside on impulse, drawn by the perfect blanket of snow in the field, the fine horse-chestnut trees in the middle of it all still weighed down by their bounty of conkers.

He wasn't even sure what had made him stop, didn't normally notice his surroundings that much. But even the most hardened cynic—and some would say he was one!—couldn't remain untouched by the beauty of the Lake District, even in November, and Jordan had finally succumbed to the perfection of this snowy-white field, pulling his car over to the side of the road before crossing over the verge and walking across the crunchy snow.

'Tim, if you do that again, we're going home,' that voice complained huskily.

He certainly hadn't expected to stumble across a pair of lovers in the snow! Surely they could have chosen somewhere a little more comfortable—and dry!—for their meeting?

So much for his impulse. What was that saying—he couldn't remember it exactly, but something to do with 'stopping along the way to smell the roses'? The season was all wrong but, even so, the first time in years he had done something so completely out of character, and he almost fell over a couple of lovers in a passionate tryst!

He decided to chance a glance at the couple, trapped as he was among the foliage. He didn't want to be caught here if the couple decided to go any further in their lovemaking!

Identical red bobble-hats were pulled low over their ears to keep out the cold, blue duffel coats buttoned up to the throat, blue jeans tucked into black wellington boots.

The two *boys* might almost have been twins except that the one on the right was taller by at least a foot. But the faces beneath the red woollen hats were both finely drawn, almost delicate-looking, a smattering of freckles across small pointed noses. Obviously the two of them were brothers. The village of Grasmere wasn't too far from here, so they had probably escaped up here to play.

As the taller of the two boys held out a conker suspended on a piece of string, the reason for his earlier protests became obvious: his opponent, now wielding a slightly larger conker, didn't pull his punches!

Jordan felt a constriction in his chest, a yearning for—for what? he scorned himself. How could he possibly feel wistful for something that had never been his?

The larger of the brothers had his conker smashed into pieces with the first forceful strike this time, shaking his head when the younger suggested they thread another conker on to his string and have a re-match. From the look of the broken conkers at their feet, the older boy had suffered a humiliating defeat.

He pocketed the knotted string before bending down to pick up a handful of snow, quickly moulding it into shape before launching it at his unsuspecting brother.

The snowball fight that followed was fast and furious, with both opponents collapsing into each other's arms in a fit of the giggles after five minutes, their clothing, hats, and faces covered in melting snow, mittens protecting their hands from the worst of the cold.

Once again Jordan felt that tug inside, these two young boys' pleasure in each other's company evoking feelings of deprivation inside him, feelings he had tried so hard to fight over the last two years, but which were becoming more and more difficult, rather than easier, to dampen down as time went on.

If he was honest, and it seemed he had to be, that had been one of the reasons he had wanted to get away for a while. Rhea-Jane and Raff were wonderful, couldn't have made him feel more wanted, but he was still a third person, who had to be an intrusion into the intimacy of their lives.

So he had chosen to come away on this business trip himself rather than sending one of his assistants. It was probably going to be a waste of his time, but it was a valid excuse to get away at least. He had even felt guilty about needing the excuse, knowing it was ridiculous, but Rhea-Jane, his well-meaning young sister, tended to be over-protective of him since she had married Raff, not wanting him to be on his own now that she had moved out of the home they had shared in London since their parents died. She had even gone so far—horror of horrors!—as to introduce him to several women she thought might make him a suitable wife.

He *didn't* want a wife, suitable—whatever that might be!—or otherwise!

But he wanted *something*, he was willing to acknowledge that. Something. And he didn't know what it was—just knew he had an aching inside of him, an emptiness that couldn't be filled by Rhea-Jane and Raff, or their darling daughter Diana, and certainly not by some woman presented to him as suitable wife material!

These two boys, as they played together so innocently, somehow had, for all Jordan's wealth and comfortable lifestyle, so much more than he did. But at thirty-two he could hardly expect that same anticipation of the promise of the future that such youth was bound to have. Indeed, he wondered if he had ever had it.

The two boys were brushing the snow from themselves now, their faces aglow, grinning with the satisfaction of the battle.

The older boy glanced at a watch that seemed to be hidden between the cuff of his duffel coat and the snow-damp mitt; hopefully it was a waterproof one, or he would be in trouble when he got home!

'We had better get back.' He spoke in a voice that, although husky, didn't seem to have broken yet, but perhaps he was a little young for that.

The younger boy made a face. 'Oh, do we have to?' he protested.

His brother looked regretful. 'You know we do.'

'I suppose so.' The younger one sighed, not at all enthusiastic.

'Come on,' the older boy encouraged brightly. 'I'll race you back!'

The challenge had no sooner been offered than it was taken up, the smaller boy turning—luckily in the opposite direction to where Jordan still stood!—and running off towards the village.

Jordan watched as his brother deliberately gave him a good head start before giving chase.

Jordan was finally able to emerge from his hiding-place, well aware that in London his behaviour would have been looked upon with suspicion. Who would understand the explanation that he had been gazing upon a stolen childhood?

Was that really what he was looking for? Of course not, he chided himself. That time had gone and could never be given back to him.

As the two boys had gone by the time he looked in the direction they had run off to. Except for their footprints in the snow, the disturbed snow from their snowball fight, they might never have been here at all.

Except that seeing them had had an effect on Jordan that couldn't be dismissed as easily. That aching emptiness inside him was becoming so vast it was starting to control him rather than the other way around.

The last thing he felt like doing was going on with the business of visiting, and being charming to, the aged spinster Miss Grace Brown. She was sure to be a fluffy old dear who couldn't even begin to deal with a businessman of his calibre, and the idea of talking her into selling the 'ancient pile' that had probably been in her family for generations, so that he might make it into a leisure complex, somehow now left a nasty taste in his mouth. Most of the people who knew him—or thought they did—wouldn't recognise this emotion in him at all, would think he had gone soft. And maybe he had.

He gave one last wistful glance in the direction the two boys had taken, before turning on his heel and walking purposefully back towards his parked car, the mantle of Jordan Somerville-Smythe firmly back in place.

Or almost...

CHAPTER ONE

MISS GRACE BROWN, when she came in answer
to the jingling bell that could be heard in the
depths of the house after he had pulled the bell-
rope outside, was exactly as Jordan had imagined her to be from the letters she had sent to
his solicitors in reply to their correspondence
concerning selling her home: small and delicate,
with fluffy white hair caught back in an untidy
bun at her nape, sparkling—but faded in
colour—blue eyes in a face that had once been
beautiful, the pink twin-set accompanied by the
customary string of pearls about her throat, her
skirt the expected tweed, as her shoes were the
expected brown brogues.

The house was as he had imagined too from
the reports—huge, old, and dilapidated. But it
did have extensive grounds, and a house could
be renovated, made to be what you wanted it to
be. As in a leisure complex...

At the moment this elderly lady ran it as a sort
of boarding house, although she seemed to have
only two permanent guests, with the occasional
casual visitor during the summer months. There
was hardly enough income there, his sources re-
ported, to keep the place ticking over on a day-

to-day basis. By the look of the threadbare carpet in the hallway behind Grace Brown, and the emulsioned rather than papered walls, that income didn't keep things 'ticking over' very well.

'Good afternoon.' She smiled up at him brightly, her movements birdlike, even her voice light and a little girlish. 'Come in.' She opened the door wider, turning to walk down the hallway where a light already glowed in the gloomy interior despite the efforts of the bright emulsion. 'We've been expecting you, of course.' She shot him another smile over her shoulder.

'You have?' Jordan frowned; David, his personal assistant, had already made the blunder of misplacing their main file on Charlton House and its inhabitants—if he had now also warned them of Jordan's arrival here, then Jordan had seriously misjudged him. Arriving here unannounced had been his only advantage without the benefit of that file!

'Do come in.' She turned at the end of the hallway to reveal a little reprovingly, 'You're letting in a draught!'

Suitably chastened, Jordan entered the house and quickly closed the door behind him. It wasn't much warmer inside than it had been out!

Miss Brown waited for him to reach her before turning into a sitting-room, a room that was shabbily welcoming, the worn sofa and four armchairs of differing patterned brocade, the carpet in here even more threadbare than the one in the hallway, in a pattern of faded pink and cream flowers.

There was too much furniture in the room, several tables, one with a chess-set on top of it, the pieces left about the board, as if the two players had been disturbed mid-game. And yet there was no one else in the room.

A tall old-fashioned standard-lamp stood beside the chair nearest the fireplace, alight, but really adding little to the illumination of the room. An old piano, its dark brown wood scourged with scratches, stood against one wall, the lid raised above the keys, a music sheet open on its stand, again giving the impression that someone had been playing it recently but been disturbed.

A fire gleamed in the darkened fireplace, logs crackling warmly.

It was a room totally unlike any Jordan had ever been in before, and yet just being here gave him a warm feeling inside, as if he had finally come home . . .

Miss Brown was looking up at him curiously. 'You're very late, you know.' She made it a statement rather than a reprimand, smiling sweetly.

Jordan was still dazed at the strange feeling that had enveloped him as soon as he entered the house, the cut-throat world he existed in in London fading into the background as if it had never been.

'I am?' he said uninterestedly.

'Very.' She frowned. 'Nick was sure you weren't coming,' she added sadly.

Jordan drew his attention from the yellow flames in the fireplace with effort, resisting, for the moment at least, the sudden urge he had to stretch out in one of the armchairs and fall asleep. 'Nick?' he prompted, fighting to control these feelings of lethargy that was such anathema to his usual character; he hadn't taken a holiday in years, let alone felt lethargic!

She nodded, giving him a coy smile. 'He boards here,' she explained trilly. 'But he's a little shy about meeting new people. He was playing the piano until you rang the doorbell. And he plays so well too,' she added wistfully.

Jordan instantly felt as if he had deprived this sweet little woman of a special treat, realising now that Nick must be one of the permanent boarders here. 'I'm sorry——'

'Don't be.' She dismissed the mood of melancholy that had swept over her as quickly as it had first appeared, smiling again now, her emotions erratic, to say the least, Jordan decided.

His solicitors hadn't mentioned that Miss Grace Brown, as well as owning Charlton House, was also a little strange!

'Nick will soon get used to you,' she told him confidently, squeezing his arm reassuringly.

Jordan gave a frown; he didn't think he was going to be here long enough for anyone to 'get used' to him.

Which was a pity...

Even Rhea-Jane, who, as sisters went, was one of the best, couldn't help but be surprised at the unexpected feelings of homecoming he felt in this house, wouldn't understand his feelings at all. He wasn't altogether sure *he* did!

He straightened his shoulders beneath the navy blue overcoat that was accepted wear among his contemporaries in town, but which, he realised, looked far too formal here. 'If we could get down to business——'

'Oh, you don't want to talk to me about that,' the tiny birdlike woman told him teasingly.

Jordan's frown deepened. No one had told him that Grace Brown had a business adviser. According to the last report he had, *she* had flatly refused to consider any offer for her home; in fact she hadn't even wanted to hear about it.

It seemed that someone had been a little remiss all round concerning Miss Grace Brown and Charlton House!

She picked up some letters from one of the coffee-tables. 'You'll need to talk to Grace about that,' she smiled. 'I have to take down the post that arrived today, so if she's in the kitchen I'll tell her you're here.'

Only one thing in that twittering speech really mattered to Jordan. '*You* aren't Grace Brown?' He hadn't spent the last ten minutes talking to a complete stranger, had he—a stranger, moreover, who was 'strange', in the nicest possible way, of course, but definitely a little odd, if harmless enough?

'Goodness, no!' She laughingly dismissed the very thought of that. 'Although it's nice of you to think so, Mr Gregory.'

Mr Gregory? Who the hell was——?

'I'm Jessica Amery.' She held out one tiny hand to be shaken. 'But everyone calls me Jessie.'

The other permanent boarder here, Jordan realised frustratedly, deliberately keeping the grip light, afraid he might crush her fragile bones in his much stronger hand. He shook his head. 'I think there must be——'

'You know,' she gave him a rather piercing look from beneath silvery brows, releasing her hand slowly, 'I always tend to judge a man by his handshake.'

Oh, dear, and his rather limp grasp hadn't found favour, he was sure.

But once again she had interrupted him when he had been about to correct her mistake concerning his own identity; he didn't know who this Mr Gregory was, but he certainly wasn't him. Although the mistake in identity at least explained a lot of her earlier remarks; they hadn't been meant for him at all, but for the absent Mr Gregory. The other man would probably find himself being addressed as Mr Somerville-Smythe when he did at last arrive, just to add to the confusion!

And no one deserved to be saddled with that name unless they had to be, Jordan thought with bitterness.

'Everyone calls me Jordan,' he invited dully, wondering how long before, or indeed if, he was going to be reconciled to the past.

'Jordan,' Jessie repeated brightly. 'We all wondered what the "J" stood for,' she nodded.

Whether from approval, he wasn't sure. But the mix-up in names seemed to be getting a little out of hand. 'I——'

'Ah, I think that must be Grace now.' Jessie tilted her head to one side as she listened to the slamming of the front door. 'I thought she was in the kitchen preparing dinner. That means the meal is going to be late.' She frowned. 'Unless we're having salad. But we wouldn't be having salad on a day like this. I wonder——'

'Jessie. Miss Amery,' Jordan cut in a little impatiently. Really, Jessie was charming, in small doses, and he was sure the subject of what she was being served for dinner was of interest to her; she didn't give the impression that her life was a hot-bed of new and wild experiences. But this habit she had of wandering from the point could be more than a little irritating, especially when because of it he had spent the last ten minutes believing he was talking to someone else entirely! 'I think perhaps I ought to meet Miss Brown,' he suggested pointedly.

'Grace?' Jessie blinked a little dazedly. 'Is she here?'

'She just came in—remember?' Jordan prompted as muffled voices could be heard in the hallway, making a move towards the door.

'So she did,' the elderly lady recalled happily. 'She will be so pleased you've arrived at last.'

And he would be glad when he could talk to someone who would understand the mistake there had been about his identity!

'Grace? Grace!' Jessie reached the door ahead of him, quick on her feet in spite of her years, stepping lightly out into the hallway. 'He's here! And we were all wrong—his name is Jordan,' she announced excitedly.

Quite what Grace Brown's initial reaction to this was Jordan had no idea, the other woman still being out in the hallway. He could only hope Miss Grace Brown wasn't as scatty as the irrepressible Jessie, or he was going to be explaining himself forever!

His eyes widened incredulously as it wasn't an elderly lady who entered the room but a young boy of about seven with a blaze of bright red hair, his gaze distinctly critical as he looked up at Jordan.

'Jordan!' he finally said disgustedly. 'I said you were a Jeremy. Jessie said it had to be John——'

'Because it's one of my favourite names,' the elderly lady explained dreamily.

'Nick chose James,' the young boy continued as if he hadn't been interrupted at all, probably used to the elderly lady's habit of deviating from the real point of the conversation, Jordan decided.

Jordan had no idea who this young boy was, but he had an appealingly impish face beneath that startling red hair, his eyes more grey than blue. 'And what did Grace—Miss Brown—think?' he prompted drily, prepared, for the moment, to humour the little boy. His friends in London would be astounded at his forbearance, he realised, but his time since he had arrived here had already been one of the strangest he had ever spent; why should it stop now?

'I refused to play guessing games with something as important as a person's name,' remarked a husky voice from the doorway.

Miss Grace Brown at last!

No, not Grace Brown but the elder brother of the two Jordan had been watching less than an hour ago...

The wellington boots had gone now, showing the denims tucked into thick black woollen socks. But the duffel coat was the same, and so was the red bobble-hat, the elfin features that so matched the younger boy's in the room the same, too, Jordan now realised.

A glance at the little boy revealed the red woollen hat stuffed into one of the pockets of his duffel coat, the dark mittens into the other.

Then *where* was Grace Brown? he wondered
frustratedly. Even as he tried to look past the
elder brother out into the hallway behind him,
the boy lifted a hand and removed the red woollen
hat. Jordan couldn't hold back his gasp as a riot
of deep red curls fell down about the slender
shoulders to surround the tiny features covered
with that smattering of freckles.

Not a boy at all, but a young girl, a girl so
startlingly lovely that she took Jordan's breath
away!

'But if I had made a guess——' the girl came
further into the room, dark grey eyes thoughtful
'—I would have said—Joshua!' she announced
with satisfaction.

Not just any young girl, it appeared, but *Miss
Grace Brown*!

And not an elderly lady either, but a young
woman of probably nineteen or twenty. He had
assumed from the old-fashioned name, and the
circumstances under which she lived, that Grace
Brown was elderly. But he realised now that no
one had actually said she was.

This young woman was ethereally lovely, long
dark lashes surrounding the most beautiful
smoky grey eyes he had ever seen, red hair so
thick and luxuriantly lovely that Jordan had to
clench his hands into fists at his sides to stop
himself from reaching out and burying them in
that fiery magnificence.

This simply wasn't like him. Oh, he had his relationships with women, beautiful women, but they had always been convenient arrangements for both of them, with very little actual emotion involved. He could never before remember an instantaneous response like this to any woman, let alone one who looked so delicately young.

He didn't know what was happening to him!

He didn't look like a Joshua, Grace had to admit ruefully. Not that she was sure *what* a Joshua would look like, but this tall, distinguished man with his expensively tailored clothing, short-styled dark hair and cobalt-blue eyes somehow wasn't a Joshua.

Because he was a Jordan. Although he looked more than capable of 'knocking down a few walls' if he chose to!

Grace looked at him consideringly. A stern man, she would guess by the harsh lines beside his nose and mouth. But forthright too, she would say, from the directness of that dark blue gaze. He had beautiful eyes, the darkest blue, and yet with that intense light behind them. She had seen a car that colour once, had commented on the beauty of its colour to Timothy; he had been absolutely disgusted with her for liking the *colour* of the car and not realising it was a Porsche! What she knew about cars, the expensive kind or any other, could be written on the back of a postage stamp.

Although as she and Timothy had walked up to the house a few minutes ago even she had recognised the sleek green model parked outside in the driveway as a Jaguar; even she knew what a Jaguar looked like. It was because Timothy had spotted the car that the two of them had come in the front door at all; they would usually have gone down the back stairs straight into the kitchen. But they had both been curious as to who their visitor was.

Jordan.

Why was he here?

There was something in the depths of his eyes, she realised compassionately, that same bewilderment she had known after the death first of her mother giving birth to Timothy, and then of her father eighteen months ago from a heart-attack. Jordan had known a similar loss; she could sense that.

He also looked a little dazed at the moment!

Jessie: darling, muddle-headed Jessie. Grace smiled fondly at the elderly lady; what had she been doing with the poor man while he waited for them to come home?

'What are we having for dinner, Grace?' Jessie looked at her anxiously.

Ah, so that was what they had been discussing. Or, at least, one of the things, Grace correctly read from Jordan's rueful expression. She knew herself how erratic Jessie's conversation could be, but she was a dear, none the less. And she did have a passion for her food. And why not, when her only child, a son, only ever came to see her with the intention of trying to talk her into going into a home? Food didn't hurt her. Grace smiled at the elderly lady affectionately. 'I put a casserole in the oven before I went to collect Tim from school,' she assured her.

Jessie's face instantly brightened. 'You're such a warm, considerate girl, Grace. There you are, Mr Gregory——'

'Jordan,' he put in abruptly.

Grace looked at him concernedly; he really was very tense. And extremely attractive, those dark blue eyes mesmerising, she had to admit. But also filled with that bewildered pain and disillusionment...

'Oh, thank you, Jordan.' Jessie clasped his hand warmly. 'And you must call me Jessie,' she invited with a coy smile. 'And how lovely for you, now that you've at last arrived, that you should get here in time for dinner. Grace is such a wonderful cook,' she added effusively.

'Chicken casserole is hardly cordon bleu, Jessie,' Grace said drily. 'I'm sure Mr—Jordan,' she amended at his sharp-eyed look, 'is used to much more exciting fare——'

'How long before dinner is ready, Grace?' Timothy cut in, his eyes bright.

She eyed her little brother suspiciously; he wasn't usually concerned with punctuality where meals were concerned. 'Half an hour or so...' she told him questioningly.

He turncd excitedly to the tall man now standing beside the fireplace. 'Would you take me for a drive in your car before dinner?'

'Timothy!' she gasped incredulously, looking awkwardly across the room at Jordan.

Her brother looked slightly rebellious. 'But I've never been in a Jag, and——'

'Jaguar, Timothy,' she corrected quietly, still a little taken aback at this uncharacteristic show of bad manners; obviously the lure of the thought of a drive in a Jaguar superseded everything she had tried to teach him about politeness! 'And I'm sure Jordan would much rather go up to his room and unpack before dinner.' She turned to the man as he watched them so intently. 'The room has been aired, even though you are two days later than you expected to be in your original letter——'

'I——'

'But, of course, I realise you weren't a hundred per cent sure about the twenty-fifth as your day of arrival.' She smiled to take away any rebuke he might have read into her earlier words. 'I'm not that strict about arrival dates,' she said, and shook her head. 'And I don't exactly have people beating a path to the door this time of year!' Or the rest of the year really, although they did pick up the occasional summer visitor looking for solitude rather than luxurious accommodation;

the latter she certainly couldn't offer here! But Jordan was a 'winter visitor' in search of solitude.

Jordan looked at her wordlessly for several seconds, blue gaze piercing, flickering away with a vulnerability that was vaguely endearing. He seemed undecided. Which Grace guessed was an unfamiliar emotion to him. He had aroused her curiosity about him in spite of herself.

'Oh, please take me for a drive in your car!' Timothy was the one to break the silence, gazing imploringly up at Jordan. 'I've never been in a Jaguar before,' he added, eyes wide with anticipation, and Grace could already hear the tales he would tell his schoolfriends about the adventure in the morning.

Jordan was looking almost wistfully at Timothy now, Grace thought, her own frown thoughtful. He was an enigma, this man Jordan. And she felt an intense curiosity to know more about him.

'Did you enjoy your snowball fight earlier?' He was talking to Timothy now, his tone gentle.

Grace looked at him sharply, wondering how he could possibly know—she hadn't realised anyone had watched them earlier, but how else could this man know about the snowball fight if he hadn't actually seen them have it?

Timothy gave the grin of the victor. 'Grace isn't bad at snowballing, for a girl,' he shrugged.

'Timothy Brown, you only won at all because you played dirty and put one down my neck!' she rebuked good-naturedly.

Jordan watched her intently. 'You run this house alone, Miss Brown?'

'Grace,' she corrected as automatically as he had earlier, knowing that what he was really asking was where her parents were, that she should have the responsibility of Timothy plus the running of a big house like this one. From the intentness of his gaze she had a feeling he had intended disarming her with the unexpectedness of the question, knew herself matched with a sharp intelligence. 'I manage,' she dismissed, her gaze steady.

Jordan met that gaze. 'I'm sure you do,' he acknowledged quietly.

She straightened. 'And right now I had better take off the rest of these damp things and finish cooking dinner,' she said brightly, knowing that although the two of them knew little about each other they at least understood each other; Grace was here 'managing' this house because circumstances had dictated that she do so, and because they had she did it with all the love and care that she could. Jordan was here for reasons of his own, but those reasons owed just as much to circumstances as her own.

Timothy was still looking up at Jordan with hopefully expectant eyes. Grace knew that look only too well, had succumbed to the pleading there too many times herself not to know it. And she could see Jordan wasn't unmoved by the pleading over-big eyes either.

'If you would like to bring your things in from the car I'll show you up to your room...?' she politely prompted Jordan, removing her scarf.

He was looking at her again now, indecision in the dark blue depths of his eyes. She smiled at him, knowing instinctively that the vulnerability she sensed in him wasn't a part of himself he felt able to cope with.

Grace doubted he would be able to cope with her response to that either; he didn't look as if he very often had women he was barely acquainted with throw their arms around him because they felt an overwhelming need to comfort him in whatever pain it was he was suffering!

There was an answering flicker of warmth in the dark blue depths of his eyes, although he barely smiled in response to hers. She wondered what he would look like if he ever laughed. Younger, was her instant guess. He had an air about him of someone much older than the early thirties she guessed him to be. Too much responsibility at too young an age, she surmised, wondering if she had a similar air herself.

She didn't think so, because she wasn't unhappy. And this man obviously was. Very unhappy.

'I haven't brought much with me,' he finally answered in measured tones. 'But I'll bring it in after I've taken Tim for his drive,' he added decisively.

Any reply Grace might have made to this remark was drowned out by Timothy's whoop of delight and his cries for them to go right now, this very second. Just in case Jordan should change his mind, Grace guessed with affection.

Jordan stood across the room with Timothy's hand clinging determinedly to his much larger one, awkwardly so, as if the trust in him this young child showed came as a shock. 'Is that all right with you?' He looked at Grace enquiringly.

'Of course,' she nodded, smiling at her brother as he beamed his excitement up at her. 'Behave yourself,' she warned indulgently.

He replied in the affirmative, but in truth it was obvious he barely heard her remark, his thoughts already transfixed on driving in the back seat of a Jaguar. Compared to the old Mini Grace drove him about in he would feel like royalty, the leather interior of the car parked outside being plush to say the least.

She watched them walk to the door together, the tall dark-haired man, and the small red-haired boy who was the centre of her world.

She had known from the day her father died so suddenly and left Timothy in her sole care that she would always do everything she could to ensure that her brother's world would be as secure as she could make it for him. As she stood and watched Jordan and Timothy walk out to the car side by side she had a vague feeling of disquiet, as if *her* world would never be quite the same again from this moment on...

CHAPTER TWO

WHAT the hell was he *doing*?

He should have told them exactly who he was the moment he realised the mistake there had been over identity. But something had held him back from doing that. Jordan deliberately pushed the image of dark grey eyes surrounded by long dark lashes to the back of his mind.

He was here, in Grace Brown's home—a Grace Brown who had turned out to be far from the elderly spinster he had expected to meet—under a false identity, and false pretences.

He looked about the room he had been given for his stay—or rather, J. Gregory had been given! It was as worn and faded as the rest of the house, but it was clean and comfortable, and somehow homely and welcoming.

There was another flowered carpet on the floor, green this time, cream-coloured paper on the walls, and Jordan hadn't seen a candlewick bedspread like the one on the double bed that took up most of the room for years, the convenience of duvets not seeming to have entered this old-fashioned household.

The bathroom was down the hallway, something he definitely wasn't used to, and yet he felt

33

at home here already. Rhea and Raff were going to think he had taken leave of his senses, but he intended staying on here.

He would have to telephone them, of course, otherwise they were likely to send out a search-party after a couple of days. And, as he was here as a 'Mr Gregory', the last thing he wanted was for them to do that.

Mr J. Gregory...

The other man had obviously changed his mind about coming here after all, and hadn't bothered to let Grace Brown know that. At least, Jordan hoped that was what had happened. He was going to look worse than ridiculous if the real Mr Gregory should turn up after all. Especially as he would then have to tell them who he really was.

Oh, hell! He should leave here now, he knew he should. And yet somehow he couldn't do it, felt at peace for the first time in a very long time. Over two years, in fact.

Two years... Since he had discovered the man whom he had always believed to be his father wasn't his father after all.

It had been the merest chance that his sister Rhea had met Raff Quinlan in the first place. Fate, Rhea called it.

And the secrets that had emerged after that meeting had shattered Jordan's world forever.

Rhea was married to Raff now, and they had a beautiful daughter Diana, with Rhea's red hair and Raff's serious charm, but for the last two years Jordan had been avoiding facing the confusion and pain he felt about even his own identity. He wasn't really Jordan Somerville-Smythe, had no right to that name, and yet, if he wasn't Jordan Somerville-Smythe, who was he?

He wasn't sure any more. The Lake District, this house, seemed a strange place to begin to find the answer to that, and yet this was the first time he had felt truly relaxed in years. He couldn't leave now even if he wanted to.

Besides, he excused his own actions, his curiosity had been well and truly aroused now. The boy, Tim, had talked incessantly when Jordan had taken him for the promised drive in his car, but he hadn't seemed to find the fact that he lived in this huge house with his sister, Jessie Amery, and the elusive Nick—the other man had still been absent when Jordan had returned with Tim a short time ago—interesting enough to go into in great detail.

It was a very strange household for a young woman of the nineteen or twenty Jordan had guessed Grace to be. A girl of those tender years should be out enjoying herself with other people her age, but Grace didn't give the impression she in the least resented the responsibilities she had.

In fact, she had a calmness and serenity that Jordan envied...

*   *   *

What a strange mixture of contradictions her new boarder was, Grace mused as she set the dinner out on the big tray ready to take upstairs to the dining-room—where hopefully Timothy would have laid the table for their meal by now.

Jordan looked a stern, uncompromising man, as if he wouldn't suffer fools gladly, and yet he had given in to the whim of a child good-naturedly enough. Timothy hadn't yet been able to stop his bubbling excitement over being driven about in a Jaguar, his face aglow still with the pleasure of it.

When she had shown Jordan into his room a short time ago she had been quite able to see its clean shabbiness through his eyes, knew from the very look of him that this couldn't be the class of place he was used to staying in.

And yet she also knew, instinctively, that he didn't want to leave.

She only hoped his presence here wasn't going to be too disruptive to the rest of the household, wondered, curiously, what he and Nick were going to make of each other.

Jessie was already seated at the dining-room table when Grace entered with the laden tray, and Grace knew it wasn't that the elderly lady was particularly greedy, or even that she would eat a lot of the meal anyway—her appetite was birdlike—it was just that mealtimes were the most sociable times of the day for Jessie, who spent a lot of her time alone. Nick kept to his room a lot, Timothy was at school during the day, and Grace had her part-time job at the library to go to every morning during the week and had work to catch up on when she was at home. Breakfast and dinner were really the only times all of them were together.

She smiled at Jessie. 'Ready at la——' She broke off with a start as Jordan stepped out of the shadow of the bay-window across the room, her smile returning as she realised who it was.

He still wore the trousers to the suit he had been wearing earlier, and the cream shirt, but he had pulled on an Aran sweater over the latter, emphasising the fitness of his body, and darkening his skin.

From the small overnight bag he had finally brought in with him Grace had a feeling the Aran jumper was the only other clothing he had brought with him, giving the impression he hadn't intended staying long. The thought made her frown.

'Is something wrong?'

She looked up to find Jordan watching her intently, doing her best to shake off the sudden heaviness that seemed to have descended over her mood. It was ridiculous, she didn't even know this man, so why should the thought of his leaving have any effect on her?

Because he was another of her lame ducks, her father would have pointed out affectionately. As a child she had always been bringing home birds and animals that had been abandoned or injured, taking care of them until they could fend for themselves.

It had been a trait her father had believed she had carried on into adulthood, pointing out Jessie as a prime example of her compassion. And maybe she was, Jessie's son Peter making no secret of where he thought she should live, but Jordan hardly fitted into the same category. Although perhaps he did in a different way; she didn't think she was wrong about the emotional pain she glimpsed in his eyes at unguarded moments.

'No, nothing,' she answered him brightly, straightening. 'I'm glad you seem to be finding your way about the house so easily.' She had a feeling there was very little that this man wasn't completely in control of in his life!

He shrugged, as if to say he had found no difficulty with the problem. As, indeed, he probably hadn't, Grace acknowledged ruefully.

She frowned as she set the food dishes down the centre of the table so that they might each help themselves to what they wanted of the casserole and vegetables. 'Timothy seems to have missed laying a place——'

'Nick won't be coming down to dinner,' Jessie told her disappointedly—Nick being a favourite with her, she had tidied her hair and powdered her cheeks before coming down for the meal.

Grace couldn't say she was surprised at Nick's decision, had half guessed what would happen when he had made himself scarce on Jordan's arrival.

She put one of the warmed plates back on the tray, starting to take the lids off the steaming bowls of food. 'Timothy?' she called as she began, absently, to spoon food on to the plate she had put back on the tray.

'I'm here, Grace.' He came bouncing into the room with his usual energy.

'Hands washed?' She arched dark brows teasingly.

'Yep,' he grinned.

She glanced up with a conspiratorial smile for the other adults in the room, noticing as she did so that Jordan was watching her as she put the chicken casserole and accompanying vegetables on the plate. 'For Nick,' she explained awkwardly, instantly wondering at this need she felt to explain herself to this man. 'He—often eats alone,' she added dismissively. 'Although I don't make a habit of providing food in the rooms,' she was quick to add, not wanting there to be two of them she ran up and down the stairs after. Nick was different.

Jordan nodded non-committally. 'Then I should take it up while it's hot.'

For some reason she felt irritated as she carried the tray up the stairs to Nick's room. It hadn't been so much what Jordan had said as the way

he had said it. A man accustomed to giving orders
and expecting them to be obeyed unquestioningly.

As she had just done!

Jordan was feeling more and more curious about
the man Nick. Timothy had mentioned the other
man a couple of times when they had gone for
their drive before dinner—nothing specific, but
it was significant enough, it seemed to Jordan,
that the other man should have been mentioned
at all.

And now Grace was running up the stairs with
the other man's meal on a tray because he had
decided he 'wasn't coming down to dinner'.

It was the idea of Grace having to do such
menial tasks that Jordan found he didn't like.
Which was ridiculous; *he* was probably the reason
the elderly man had disappeared into his bedroom
in the first place!

He gave Grace a rueful smile when she came
back into the room to have her own dinner, although even as he did so he realised she couldn't
possibly know the stupidity of his thoughts. The
smile felt unfamiliar, and he realised it was the
first relaxed smile he had given anyone for
months. By the widening of Grace's calm grey
eyes that was an easily recognisable fact!

'Could I use your telephone after the meal?'
He decided to change the subject altogether,
knowing he would have to telephone Rhea and
Raff tonight or they would worry he hadn't ar-

rived safely. He had only brought an overnight case with him—a fact he was sure Grace had noticed earlier!—and so the other couple would be expecting him back some time tomorrow at the latest. He would have to let them know of his change of plan, of his intention of taking a holiday in the Lake District.

'Of course,' Grace confirmed instantly. 'Timothy, don't do that with your potato, dear,' she turned to scold gently.

Jordan watched her firm gentleness with the small boy, realising it was an occupation he could become fond of.

He must be getting senile!

Maybe he needed this holiday more than he had realised. He certainly was in a reflective mood today, for him.

But the food was good, even if the conversation did consist mainly of Timothy's questioning as to his opinion on one fast car after another. Never having owned any of the exclusive models the little boy mentioned, his opinion was an unlearned one, much to Timothy's obvious disgust. He could see by the end of the meal that he had fallen a couple of notches in the little boy's estimation.

Strangely, that mattered to him very much...

His experience with children was limited to his niece Diana, but, as she was only fifteen months old, and the admiration he felt for her was more than returned, it wasn't a very good example.

Timothy, for all that he was only seven years old—another snippet of information he had given Jordan on that short drive out!—was an intelligent and discerning little boy. And, for reasons Jordan couldn't even begin to explain to himself, he wanted the two of them to get on together.

Although if he stayed on at Charlton House long, enjoying Grace's delicious cooking, he was going to put on weight!

Even at the leisure complex which Raff had made of his home, and which he and Rhea ran together, as a family they tended to eat in the hotel restaurant for convenience, and so it was months since Jordan had enjoyed the luxury of a home-cooked meal. Grace's chicken casserole had reminded him of just how good it could be.

'The telephone is in the small room, next to the sitting-room, that I use as an office,' Grace informed him as she stood up to clear away after the meal.

Jordan stood up too. 'I'll help you do this first——'

She was shaking her head even as he began to gather up the plates, firmly taking them from him. 'You're a guest here, Mr—Jordan,' she amended at his fierce look. 'This is what you pay your rent for,' she added dismissively.

And a very small amount it was too, he had learnt earlier. Jordan found it incredible to believe Grace could make any money at all from the small payment she asked for overnight accommodation and meals.

A house like this must have ten or twelve bedrooms already, and would benefit greatly by extension—could be worth a small gold-mine if it were renovated properly and run on a more businesslike basis.

His wandering thoughts had brought him back to the reason he had come to Charlton House at all. He and Raff, business partners in the luxury complex Raff had made of Quinlan House, had been searching around for another suitable house with grounds to make into a similar venture. His own personal assistant, given the task of seeking out such a property, had come up with Charlton House in the Lake District. Unfortunately, their advances to Grace Brown about selling the house to Quinlan Leisure, the name of the company Jordan and Raff ran the business under, had been rejected with a haste that had seemed pretty final. Not to be put off, Jordan had continued to correspond with Miss Grace Brown through his solicitors. She had remained adamant in her decision not to sell, which was when Jordan had decided to come up here himself to talk to her.

Taking on a false identity, which was sure to be misconstrued if discovered, seemed to have put an end to any negotiations he might have pursued in that direction himself. But for the moment he didn't care, felt more at peace with himself than he had for a long time. There was just Raff and

Rhea's minds to put at rest and then he could forget about business completely for a while. Who knew? He might even start to enjoy life again. Now that would be a novelty!

'If you're sure...' he accepted politely, much more interested in going in search of the 'office', he had to admit.

It wasn't so much an office as a private sitting-room, had the charm and neatness of Grace Brown stamped all over it. Not that the furniture or the décor in here were any more luxurious than in the room next door, because if anything the floral-covered sofa and armchair in here looked older than the furniture in the adjoining room. But they were clean, completely neat and tidy, as was the sideboard bearing several photographs, and the small dining-table Grace seemed to use as her desk, from the look of the neat piles of correspondence upon its surface. Jordan wouldn't be at all surprised if the half-dozen or so letters sent through his solicitor didn't sit among this number.

Sitting neatly in the middle of the table was the sought-after telephone. But it was to the side-board bearing the photographs that Jordan went. There were several photographs of Tim, in-stantly recognisable, from babyhood up, and, next to these, formal photographs of a man with hair as bright a red as his two offspring—for this surely had to be Grace's father—and he was laughing down into the face of the woman who stood at his side, a woman with Grace's face and yet somehow different: her mother and father, Jordan knew without a doubt.

On the other side of these was a display of ones of Grace Brown from babyhood through to adolescence and on up to the present day. In at least two of these—it was exactly two, Jordan knew without hesitation!—a tall, blond-haired man stood at her side. Tall and blond, handsome in a rakish way, several years older than Jordan himself, vaguely familiar, as if Jordan should recognise him, and yet he didn't.

What was he doing in the photographs with Grace? Could he be her boyfriend? Jordan frowned at this possibility.

'Did you manage to find the telephone?'

He turned with a guilty start at the husky sound of Grace's voice, although she didn't look accusing, just curious.

'The pictures of Timothy caught my attention,' he excused with a shrug—although it must be obvious to Grace that he hadn't been standing anywhere near the photographs of Timothy when she entered the room! 'He's a lovely child.'

'Yes,' she acknowledged indulgently, moving further into the room to pick up one of the earlier photographs of her brother. 'He was a good baby too,' she reminisced, remembering the fun she and her father had had with the contented baby

Timothy had been; it had been an outlet they had both needed after the death of her mother.

Jordan looked at her as she stood bent over the photographs, lost in memories he couldn't even begin to guess at, let alone share, her face given a warm glow from the light given off by the small lamp that stood on the sideboard.

She looked very young and vulnerable at that moment, no more than a child herself, certainly not capable of carrying all the responsibilities she seemed to have. Jordan wanted to take her in his arms and relieve her of all those responsibilities, wanted to smooth that frown from between her eyes, wanted to kiss the soft peach of those slightly parted lips—what the hell...?

Grace looked up, misunderstanding the scowl on his face, putting the photograph down with a thud. 'I'll leave you to make your call,' she excused, turning to leave.

Jordan was too dazed by his unexpected response to her seconds ago to try and stop her!

Oh, he wasn't as cold and removed from human need as his sister seemed to think he was, had been attracted to women, desired them, made love to them. But that attraction had always been to *women*, moreover women who knew exactly what sort of relationship he required of them, the relationship always terminating amicably, with perhaps an expensive gift of jewellery on his part to soften the blow of parting. These affairs had been games, with both players knowing the rules.

Grace Brown wasn't a player.

She wasn't even a woman, merely a vulnerable young girl. But a few minutes ago he had wanted her with a fierceness he could never remember experiencing before! His hand shook slightly as he reached out to pick up the receiver, needing contact with his normal life.

He should really leave here now—that would be the best thing to do before he became any more embroiled in Grace Brown's life. Before he couldn't control that desire he had had to take her in his arms and kiss her until they were both breathless.

Rhea answered the call on the private line at Quinlan House, her voice warm with recognition once he had said hello, the contentment she had found as Raff's wife evident even over the telephone. 'How did you get on?' she prompted interestedly.

'Fine,' Jordan evaded.

'And Miss Brown, is she——?'

'We'll talk about it when I get home,' he cut in curtly.

'OK,' his sister accepted easily, used to his abrupt ways.

'The thing is...' he continued. No, Jordan, *no*, he anxiously instructed himself. Tell Rhea you'll be back tomorrow, as originally planned, that you'll be back in time for lunch, dinner at the latest. 'I've decided not to come straight back,' he heard himself add lightly. 'I thought I might take a short holiday up here.'

He should leave *now*. Not tomorrow. Not in a few days' time. But *now*. He *knew* he should leave.

'We've been telling you for months to take a holiday,' Rhea said with warm approval. 'But isn't the weather a little cold up at the Lakes this time of year?'

'Possibly,' he accepted non-committally. 'But I need the break more than the warm weather.' But not *here*, he was desperately telling himself inside his head. Not anywhere near Grace Brown!

'Yes, but——'

'Rhea,' he cut in tersely, 'unlike you when you decided to flit off and not tell anyone—least of all me—where you were going, I *am* over twenty-one! And I'm taking a short holiday, so I'm not coming home just yet.' He quietly replaced the receiver as he heard her initial gasp of surprise turn into a dozen questions.

And that wasn't in the least surprising.

The time Rhea had disappeared from their home had been when she had first met Raff. And fallen in love with him. And Jordan had just repeated almost word for word what Rhea had said to him then during the one brief telephone call she had made to him to reassure him she was at least well and in no danger.

Now why had he done that?

CHAPTER THREE

WHO was Jordan telephoning? Grace wondered.
A wife, possibly. She very much doubted that he
was telephoning another man, unless it was for
business purposes, and it was well past business
hours. Although Jordan had an air about him of
being able to command attention and respect no
matter what time of the day or night it was.

And yet the guess that it was a woman he was
calling persisted. Had he had an argument with
his wife—was that why he had chosen to stay on
here when everything about him pointed to his
being used to much more luxurious accommodation when he was away from home?

But somehow he didn't *look* married. And
there was that bewildered pain in his eyes.

No, perhaps not a wife, but definitely a
woman. Grace didn't know why she believed that,
she just did. What sort of woman would a man
like Jordan be interested in? she wondered. Glo-
riously beautiful, she would guess, wondrously
sophisticated, a woman who knew all the rules.

A woman, in fact, who bore absolutely no resemblance to herself.

Now what on earth had made her think a thing
like that...?

'Grace, why are you standing all alone in the hallway?' Timothy looked up at her. 'And why do you have that funny look on your face?' He frowned at her expression.

It took the innocence of a child to make her realise how ridiculously she was behaving! She gave Timothy a rueful smile, putting her arm companionably about his shoulders. 'I was miles away,' she excused. 'I suppose I had better finish clearing away,' she added briskly, having only intended to come up here briefly to make sure Jordan had found the telephone. Although why she should doubt it she didn't know; he seemed more than capable!

Timothy was watching her with a frown. 'You don't mind Mr Gregory being here, do you?'

'Do you?' she delayed, her thoughts still in conflict concerning Jordan. It was a very uncomfortable feeling.

Her brother gave a predictable grin. 'No, I think he's great.'

She raised dark brows ruefully. 'Jordan? Or his Jaguar?' she teased.

His grin didn't falter. 'Both!' His answer was unabashed. 'The car is great,' he announced the obvious. 'And Jordan talked to me while we were driving around.'

'Did he?' she encouraged softly, turning back in the direction of the dining-room; she really would have to finish clearing away—it was getting late.

The dining-room was empty now, although Jessie had piled all the used crockery up and put it at one end of the dining-table. Timothy helped Grace with loading it on to a tray without even seeming aware that he did so; he was so used to helping out with the running of the house, much more so than other little boys his age, that he did it automatically now.

He nodded now in answer to her question, his hair gleaming redder than usual in the lamplight. 'He lives in London a lot of the time,' he revealed, eager to share his new friend. 'He has a married sister. And a baby niece. And——'

'Timothy, this list of revelations sounds more like the answers to rather personal questions to me than Jordan actually sitting having a conversation with you,' Grace cut in disapprovingly, knowing her guess was correct by the unattractive way his cheeks became flushed, his freckles more prominent. 'You know I've told you not to intrude into the privacy of the people who stay here,' she scolded disappointedly.

'Jordan didn't mind,' Timothy defended a little indignantly.

Possibly not—she had noticed a certain gentleness on Jordan's part when dealing with the young boy. But even so... She wanted to know more about Jordan herself, was intensely curious about him, but she certainly had no intention of asking Timothy what else Jordan hadn't 'minded' revealing about himself!

'Well, I don't want you to do it again,' she told her brother firmly.

'He wanted to know about us, too,' Timothy continued to defend stubbornly.

Her hand was arrested in the act of putting the salt and pepper pot on the tray with the other things, although she recovered from this revelation quickly, keeping her expression deliberately bland now. 'And just what did you tell him?' she prompted, almost dreading the answer, sure that Timothy, in his youth, had been indiscreet.

He shrugged unconcernedly. 'That I live here alone with you because Mummy and Daddy died. That you're twenty, and I'm seven. That——'

'Our life histories in a few short words, in fact!' Grace frowned her dismay. 'We don't have anything to hide, Timothy,' she told him gently, 'but you really mustn't go about revealing our personal business to a complete stranger in that——'

'He isn't a stranger, he's Jordan,' Timothy announced happily, as if that made everything perfectly all right.

There wasn't a lot Grace could say to an argument like that. And yet she didn't want Timothy confiding in Jordan. Of all people...

Jordan woke slowly, for a moment unsure what had woken him, no radio-alarm clock at his bedside blasting out the seven o'clock news as it

usually did to rouse him. And then he realised
that was because there *was* no radio-alarm clock
on the cabinet beside his bed. In fact, there was
no cabinet either!

Instead, a cup of tea, still steamingly hot, he
noticed as he focused on it, sat on the table beside
his bed. A bed that, although comfortable, was
a little soft for his normal taste. A feather mattress, in fact. He hadn't known such things still
existed. But obviously they did here. At Charlton
House.

Grace Brown's home.

And someone had been kind enough to bring
him up early morning tea. Now he knew what
had woken him. And it wasn't such early morning
either; a glance at the plain but expensive watch
on his wrist had told him it was after nine o'clock.
He couldn't remember the last time he had slept
this late. Maybe he could live with the softness
of the feather mattress after all.

The tea was still refreshingly hot when he sat
up to drink it, and someone seemed to have noticed too, probably when he had a late-night cup
of tea with them the previous evening, that he
didn't take sugar in his drinks.

Grace...

It was sightly unnerving, for a man who rarely,
if ever, let down his guard, to realise that a young
woman who had already shaken his perfectly
controlled equilibrium had probably come into
his bedroom a short time ago and seen him at

his most vulnerable—sleeping like the proverbial baby!

It was disconcerting, to say the least.

But one of the things he had noticed with some surprise when he had retired to bed the previous evening was that there were no locks on the bedroom doors. It was fine, as far as he was concerned, to treat guests like part of the family, but no locks on the bedroom doors seemed to be taking things a little too far, Jordan felt.

Not that he hadn't been perfectly well covered when Grace had come into his room with the tea; far from a restless sleeper, the bedclothes were barely disturbed by his presence beneath them. And, because he had been very conscious of the unlocked bedroom door, he had chosen to sleep in his briefs rather than completely naked as he would normally have done.

No, it wasn't that that disturbed him; he just somehow felt—emotionally exposed.

Well, it was done now, beyond his control, and so he might as well enjoy the rest of his tea, then get a wash and a shave before going downstairs in search of coffee and toast.

The thought of sitting in the cosiness of the well-scrubbed kitchen downstairs, possibly chatting to Grace as she moved effortlessly about the room, filling the space with her warm gentleness and—maybe he wouldn't bother with breakfast after all!

He needed more clothes if he was to stay on here, would drive down to Windermere and pick up a few things as soon as he was ready. He could get some coffee and toast there.

'Good morning, Jordan.' Amazingly, Grace was in the hallway when he came downstairs fifteen minutes later, apparently dusting, from the cloth in her slender hand. And she looked just as warm and beautiful this morning, in the fluffy pink jumper and fitted black skirt, as she had yesterday.

Jordan had convinced himself while he showered and shaved that he had exaggerated all that beautiful tranquillity Grace Brown seemed to carry around with her like a cloak. But he only had to look at her again to know that he hadn't!

This morning Grace looked even more beautiful, more serenely lovely than he remembered, her young face glowing healthily, from where she had recently been outside, Jordan would guess, probably taking Timothy to school.

Every time Jordan looked at her he felt as if the air had been knocked out of his lungs. And it was an experience completely beyond his control.

'Breakfast?' she suggested brightly, not seeming in the least offended that he hadn't responded to her greeting.

It hadn't been that he hadn't wanted to, only that for the moment his voice seemed to have deserted him. Only!

Maybe he was starting a cold; it would certainly explain some of the symptoms he seemed to have—voice loss, and a slightly disorientated feeling that usually went along with a fever.

He refused to even contemplate any other explanation for those feelings!

Grace had already turned in the direction of the stairs that led down to the kitchen, seeming unaware of Jordan's inner conflict. 'I hope you like tea first thing in the morning?' She talked quietly, filling in for his obvious silence. 'I thought you would rather just be left to sleep until you woke up, but Jessie insisted on bringing a drink up to your room while I took Timothy to school.' She turned briefly to give him an apologetic smile.

Jessie? *Jessie* had been the one to enter his bedroom with the cup of tea. So much for his earlier disquiet!

He felt rather foolish now, didn't think the elderly, vague lady would have been in the least interested in what he looked like in bed!

And why should he have assumed Grace would be any more interested? Apart from giving him those long, searching looks occasionally, she had shown little interest in him: Which was understandable, he supposed; he was twelve years older than her, after all.

'The tea was very welcome,' he found his voice at last. 'And I was very grateful she brought it up when she did,' he added lightly, more harshly

than perhaps he meant to, but the feeling of fool-
ishness was still very much with him. 'I never
sleep late.' Now he was being pompous, he realised with an inward groan; he *had* slept late
this morning. He had to get himself back in
control of this situation!

But to refuse breakfast now, when Grace had
obviously been waiting to cook it for him, everything out ready on the work-top, the wooden table
in the centre of the large room set with one place,
wouldn't just have been rude, but churlish too.

He didn't usually bother with a full breakfast,
but, as bacon began to sizzle appetisingly in the
pan, coffee to percolate, and bread to toast, the
sudden hunger he felt told him he would have no
trouble eating the cooked breakfast today.

As he had known she would, Grace chatted
lightly as she worked, about the area and her
neighbours, and Jordan found himself just enjoying watching her as she moved about the
room, her hands long and delicate, and yet obviously capable, her movements economically ef-
ficient, her fiery red hair framing the elfin face
dominated by large grey eyes, a relaxed curve to
the shell-pink of her lips.

Jordan could never remember just enjoying
sitting looking at a woman before. He could never
remember having the time before!

Although he had a feeling, dangerously so, that
just sitting looking at Grace Brown could become
a compulsive pastime for him...

Did she have a smut on the end of her nose? A cobweb in her hair from where she had been dusting earlier? Had only remembered to put one earring in—something she regularly did? Why *was* Jordan watching her over the top of his coffee-mug in that way? Grace wondered self-consciously.

He looked less strained this morning, some of the bewilderment starting to fade from his eyes. The Aran sweater was casual, although she noticed the dark blue trousers were still the ones from the suit he had been wearing the day before. But the small overnight case he had finally brought in last night couldn't have held much more than the sweater, a change of underwear, and some toilet things.

She put the laden plate down on the table in front of him, aware that any responses he *had* made to her inconsequential chatter—and there hadn't been many!—had been monosyllabic; Jordan obviously wasn't a morning person. 'I'll leave you to enjoy your meal in peace,' she excused lightly.

'You don't have to do that,' he surprised her by saying—and then looked slightly surprised by the protest himself! He turned away. 'I don't want to drive you out of your own kitchen,' he muttered. 'I'm sure I've inconvenienced you enough for one day by coming down so late.'

There was something so endearing about this man. Grace couldn't help wondering when anyone had last held him in their arms and told him he was loved. She could be completely wrong, of course, but she had a feeling it was a very long time. Although Timothy had said he had a sister, so he must have a family who loved him somewhere.

'It's what I'm here for,' she assured him lightly.

He frowned, as if he didn't particularly care for the idea, his next remark seeming to confirm the impression. 'This is a very odd life for someone of your age.'

'Someone my age with a seven-year-old brother to bring up,' she added pointedly. 'I'm sure Timothy told you yesterday a little of our life here together,' she said challengingly; he had to know that she was aware he had been questioning the young boy.

Dark blue eyes became shuttered. 'He said you also work part-time in the local library?'

She nodded, not at all surprised he should know this. 'Ten till one, Monday to Friday. In fact,' she looked at her wristwatch, 'I should be leaving for there now.'

'I'll drive you,' Jordan instantly offered.

'You haven't finished your breakfast,' she pointed out gently.

He looked down at the food on his plate as if he had forgotten it was there. 'No—of course not. I—I'll see you later, then.' He turned away, determinedly keeping his head downbent.

Grace watched him for several seconds longer, before giving a slight shrug and leaving the room. She really did have to finish off and get ready for work. She had made a point, since getting the job two years ago when Timothy started school, of always being punctual and reliable. As only a part-time worker her position at the library was more precarious than the full-time staff's, but, with the responsibility of Timothy to consider, and that of her boarders, she couldn't do any more hours than she did, and the more indispensable she made herself when she was there, the more chance she had, she hoped, of not losing her job if the need for fewer staff arose.

But she had better check with Nick before she left to see if there was anything he wanted while she was out; he had left his rooms even less than usual since Jordan's arrival yesterday.

Nick rented the rooms on the third floor at the top of the house; in fact they were the attic rooms, but they were the ones he preferred. By tacit agreement Grace only went in there once a week to clean, and even then she didn't tidy up the rooms; Nick thrived best on disorder, he claimed.

Although Nick usually joined them downstairs for his meals, he did have a kitchen of his own, and more often than not he would get himself toast and coffee for breakfast.

But he didn't look as if he had been long out of bed this morning when he answered the door to her knock, still wearing his old blue towelling robe, his hair in disarray.

He opened the door wider for her to enter. 'You're later than usual,' he observed tersely, sipping coffee from the mug in his hand.

Grace reached up and kissed him lightly on the cheek. 'Good morning to you too, Nick,' she teased lightly.

He looked unabashed by the gentle rebuke, shrugging as he closed the door before strolling across the room. 'I wasn't complaining,' he dismissed. 'Only observing. Besides, I haven't looked out of the window this morning yet, so I have no idea whether it's a "good" one or not!'

She pulled back the curtains in answer to that, smiling a little as Nick winced at the daylight now streaming into the room. 'It snowed a little more in the night, but everywhere looks beautiful,' she told him happily.

Nick threw himself down into one of the armchairs, making no effort to look out of the window himself. 'I find this enthusiasm you have for snow strange, to say the least,' he scowled.

Grace smiled down at him fondly. 'You just don't like fresh air of any kind!'

'There is that,' he drawled. 'How is the new lodger settling in?'

He spoke lightly enough, and yet Grace knew him well enough to realise he was disturbed at having someone new staying here, otherwise he wouldn't have mentioned the other man at all!

'Fine,' she dismissed. 'Do you want anything from town today?' She changed the subject, well aware that Nick would get out of meeting Jordan at all if he could possibly manage it.

Nick eyed her morosely. 'Tim tells me this Jordan has a fantastic car, that he comes from London, that he——'

'You really shouldn't encourage him to gossip.' Grace sighed her impatience. 'And you haven't answered my question,' she prompted a little more sharply than she would normally have done. But she was very aware that there was something she wasn't telling Nick, and it made her feel slightly defensive. Nick had become such a fixture in her life, had been here for so long, that she tended to confide in him. And yet telling him about Jordan was different...

'Actually,' Nick sprang to his feet with more energy than he usually displayed, 'I would like to come in with you this morning; there are one or two things I need to get for myself.'

She raised dark brows. 'Then you had better hurry up and get ready; I'm going to be late for work otherwise.'

'Time-watching,' he taunted before going into the adjoining bedroom to dress.

Grace didn't stay in his room waiting for him, going back downstairs. The kitchen showed no evidence of Jordan, or the breakfast he had eaten, even the pots she had used for cooking washed and put away. She somehow didn't think this was the way Jordan usually began his day!

Jessie would have gone back up to her room now, resting until Grace came back at lunchtime. The elderly lady didn't sleep well at night, so was always in need of a nap during the day. Jordan would have gone out by now, and Nick would be going with her; it appealed to her sense of order that everyone was organised for the morning.

A last check of her hair, a fresh application of lipstick, and Nick still wasn't downstairs, she realised frustratedly.

'I'm sorry, are you waiting for me after all?'

She turned to smile at Jordan as he came down the stairs, realising her mistake—that he must have been up in his room collecting his overcoat.

Her breath caught in her throat as he returned her smile, those cobalt-blue eyes warm and sensual. He had an instant command of respect, this man, but it wasn't only that about him that disturbed her, made her legs feel slightly weak...

'Grace?'

She was staring! Like a silly teenager, she was staring at him and had completely forgotten to answer his original question!

She smiled brightly. Too brightly? Oh, this was so silly, she was behaving like a gauche schoolgirl! 'I have my own car,' she thanked him. 'I'm just waiting for Nick to join me.'

'Oh, yes?' Dark blue eyes narrowed. 'I haven't met your other guest yet.'

Nick was hardly a 'guest'; none of them were, Grace thought ruefully. They were all wounded people who had found somewhere to rest and lick their wounds while their emotions healed, she realised with a start. Yes, even this man in front of her...

She shrugged dismissively. 'Nick is something of a—loner.'

'Shy, you mean,' Jordan nodded understandingly.

That wasn't what she meant at all. Nick could be scornful, sarcastic, downright rude if he thought his privacy was being invaded; but it owed nothing to shyness!

'Something like that,' Grace avoided drily, inwardly wondering what these two men would make of each other. They were both such private people, it was difficult to even hazard a guess. Maybe her newest 'guest' would cause more of an upset to the household than she had bargained for, but, the truth of the matter was, she hadn't even considered Nick's feelings yesterday when she'd first met Jordan!

'Don't let us delay you,' she advised Jordan lightly as he lingered in the hallway. 'Nick has absolutely no sense of time.' And if he didn't soon hurry up she was going to have to go without him!

Jordan gave a curt inclination of his head, as if he resented what he felt was a dismissal. 'I'll see you this evening, then.'

Grace looked at his rigidly held back as he walked down the hallway towards the front door, his reaction to what she had meant as a casual remark somehow making the conversation feel unfinished, inconclusive.

'Jordan!' she suddenly called out to him. He turned slowly, dark brows raised questioningly.

And now she didn't know what she was going to say, had just somehow felt as if their conversation was incomplete. But of course it wasn't; she was being over-sensitive, and now she had to find something to say to fill the awkward silence. 'Um—we have dinner at six o'clock,' she invented quickly, instantly disappointed in the weakness of her apparent excuse for delaying him. 'Is that too early for you?' She inwardly cringed at her own inadequacy. Really, she could have come up with something better than that!

His dark brow settled into a frown. 'Six o'clock is fine. Did I give you the impression it wasn't?' He looked puzzled.

'Er—no,' she replied truthfully. 'I was just—checking.'

Jordan shrugged dismissively. 'I certainly don't expect you to alter your routine for me.'

'That wasn't exactly what I was suggesting,' Grace told him ruefully, knowing that Jessie for one would be the first to complain if they had dinner any later, and Timothy wouldn't be long after her! 'Despite what I said last night, if you wanted something on a tray in your room a little later in the evening, I'm sure it could be arranged.'

He frowned again. 'No, I don't think so, thank you.'

Delicate colour darkened her cheeks. 'It was just a thought,' she mumbled.

'And a kind one,' he nodded. 'But I actually enjoyed the family meal last night.'

He sounded as if he weren't sure which of them should be the most surprised by this admission!

An enigma, Grace decided again as she let him leave unhindered this time. She was sure, in his normal way of life, that Jordan was a man who preferred his own company. But apparently not now. Not here.

'Penny for them,' Nick invited derisively as he came down the stairs, dressed casually as usual, his hair looking as if he might have run a comb through it. But that wasn't a certainty; he might just have smoothed it back with his hand—Nick never seemed to particularly care how he looked.

She gave him a bright, dismissive smile, picking up her coat and bag. 'I don't have the time just now to satisfy your curiosity.'

Nick easily matched his longer strides to her hurried ones. 'All this rushing about all the time, clock-watching——'

'Not now, Nick,' she warned levelly, hurrying out to her car. 'Some of us have to "clock-watch", as you call it,' she added pointedly. 'Will you just get in the car?' she ordered frustratedly over the bonnet of her Mini, as he seemed in no hurry now to stop admiring how pretty the jungle of a garden looked buried under a few inches of snow, and actually get inside the car!

'No respect for their elders, that's the trouble with some people,' he grumbled mockingly as he finally folded his length inside the vehicle.

Grace gave him a brief glance as she got in beside him. 'Older doesn't necessarily mean better.' She turned the key in the ignition. 'Respect has to be earned, not just expected as one's due.' She put the car into reverse.

'Mind the tree,' Nick warned without even attempting to look backwards.

She braked instantly, although she knew she had actually been nowhere near any of the trees edging the driveway. It had been an instinctive reaction; Nick would never let her forget the time, just after she had passed her driving test, when she had put the car into reverse instead of first gear and ended up badly damaging the Mini on the tree she had hit.

'It's just as well I love you,' she finally muttered as she drove down the driveway.

His only answer was to turn and grin at her knowingly. He was irresistible when he smiled like that, Grace decided, and she found herself grinning back at him, her bad humour forgotten.

She certainly didn't notice the green Jaguar parked on the side of the road facing in the opposite direction to the one she was driving...

So that was the elusive Nick, Jordan realised as he watched the car accelerate away. The rakishly attractive man with Grace in the photograph that stood in her small private office.

The blond hair was even longer now, and from the harsh angles of the attractive face the man was also thinner than in the photograph. But it was still the same man, Jordan was sure of it. And in the flesh he looked even more familiar.

Who was he?

More important still, what was he to Grace? Why was he staying in her home?

The two of them had looked so comfortable together, laughing over some shared joke as the Mini emerged out on to the road, not even seeming to notice him as he sat looking through a road-map trying to decide which way he should have turned to Windermere. He had passed through the small lakeside town on the way here, and yet from the look of the map he had turned the wrong way completely from the house.

What rankled the most? he questioned himself. Was it the fact that his usual sense of direction seemed to have deserted him, or was it the fact that Grace had been so engrossed with the other man she hadn't even noticed his car parked at the side of the road, let alone Jordan himself?

He must be cracking up, if he could be bothered about something so trivial, he decided. He certainly wasn't acting in character.

He barely knew Grace Brown, had only met her for the first time yesterday, and, even if he did reluctantly find himself attracted to her, he was hoping for a little too much that other men wouldn't find her equally as attractive, that she didn't have a boyfriend already.

But actually staying in her own home? Albeit in his own room. At least, Jordan assumed that was the arrangement! And the man Nick looked far from being a 'boy', was at least six or seven years older than Jordan's thirty-two.

But it was really none of his business, was it, who Grace Brown chose to go out with? Or anything else, for that matter.

Self-lecture over, he very firmly turned on the ignition, putting all thoughts of Grace Brown from his mind, concentrating on the purchases he needed to make while in Windermere.

He even fooled himself into thinking he didn't notice the fact that he deliberately drove slower than usual so that he shouldn't catch up with the Mini on the winding roads...

CHAPTER FOUR

'JORDAN GREGORY, Nick Parrish,' Grace introduced the two men at dinner that evening.

But, having persuaded Nick to join them,
having done so under duress after she had told
him she had no intention of permanently providing his meals upstairs on a tray just because
he wanted to hide out from the new guest—a
direct challenge that even Nick couldn't ignore—
she wasn't altogether sure how he was going to
behave now he was here.

One thing she was sure of, however—the two
men were more than a match for each other!

They faced each other now across the dining-
table, one so fair, the other so dark, equally
powerfully built, although they were dressed totally differently, despite the fact they were both
dressed casually. Nick wore his customary denims
and an over-big dark green sweatshirt, and
Jordan wore dark tailored trousers with a formal
shirt unbuttoned at the throat beneath a navy blue
V-necked jumper.

Clothes the latter had bought only today, Grace
felt sure.

The two men shook hands, eyeing each other
like adversaries.

Grace could understand Nick's behaving in that way; he viewed all new people with suspicion. But she didn't know why Jordan should feel so defensive. Jessie, bless her, was completely oblivious to any tension in the room, intent upon her food, and Timothy was still puffed up with his own self-importance at being able to go to school and claim his friend Jordan had a Jaguar and that he had taken him out for a drive in it! It was a gross exaggeration, considering his real relationship to Jordan, but it was what Grace had herself heard him claim as he had hurtled into the school playground this morning.

He might even be plotting right now how to get Jordan to take him out in the car again. Even worse, he may be working himself up to asking Jordan if he would take some of his schoolfriends plus himself out for a drive! Grace wouldn't put that past him, from the look of the little half-smile on his lips. She had better have a chat with this particular young man at bedtime.

But right now it seemed she was the one who would have to act as a buffer between the two men sitting so obviously silent at the table. At least, it was obvious to her!

She turned to Jordan. 'Did you have a nice day?' Hardly scintillating conversation, but it would do as a start. He shrugged dismissively, his narrowed gaze still fixed on Nick, the latter meeting that gaze challengingly.

Grace could cheerfully have hit Nick; he drew attention to himself just by his rude behaviour!

'I just picked up a few essentials in Windermere,' Jordan decided to answer her question.

Like a change of clothes, Grace guessed. In fact, probably several of them. She couldn't help wondering what had happened to change his mind about the length of his stay; he had so obviously originally intended it to be of short duration.

'This is a strange place for a man like you to choose to stay,' Nick drawled almost accusingly.

Dark blue eyes glazed over coldly, and Grace was able in those few seconds to see just how formidable Jordan could be when he chose to be. And yet he had been so kind with Timothy, infinitely gentle and considerate with her...

'"A man like me"?' he repeated in a voice that was dangerously soft.

Nick looked him over consideringly. 'You're hardly the type for a brief winter break in the Lakes,' he finally scorned.

'I'm not?' Jordan met his gaze steadily.

Neither of them was making any attempt to eat the beef pie she had made for the meal, which was a pity because, even if she said it herself, it was one of her better efforts at cooking.

'No.' Nick rested his chin on his hand as his elbow rested on the table-top. 'What *are* you doing here?'

Grace gasped out loud at the audacity of this question; Nick really was the absolute end!

Jordan looked unruffled. 'Taking ''a brief winter break in the Lakes'',' he bit out evenly. 'What's your excuse?'

Grace choked as a piece of food lodged in her throat, coughing frantically, her eyes watering. Neither man made any attempt to come to her aid, and so she gulped down her water gratefully, looking anxiously at Nick once she had regained a little of her composure, alarmed by his narrowed eyes and the tightness of his mouth.

'Here.' Jordan held out his own glass of water for her, an amused glitter in his eyes as he met her gaze.

He was enjoying Nick's challenge, she realised! He couldn't know quite the time-bomb he was walking into, but then, he didn't know Nick very well either. Yet. Grace had a feeling that was going to change very soon.

'Thank you.' She took the water more to be polite than anything else, although her coughing fit did at least seem to have diverted both men's attention, as Nick turned to her too.

'Food go down the wrong way?' he taunted, obviously wishing he had never given in to her persuasions to come down here for his dinner in the first place. She shot him a reproachful glance; he could be hard, embittered, but he wasn't usually cruel.

He was probably the most eligible bachelor in Northland;

He turned back to Jordan, his mouth tight. 'I don't need an "excuse",' he bit out harshly. 'I happen to live here!'

Jordan gave an acknowledging inclination of his head. 'And, for the moment, so do I.'

Stand-off—Grace hoped! Things could get very awkward indeed around here if these two men should decide to lock horns and continue to fight every time they saw each other; mealtimes especially could become very uncomfortable for them all.

She was aware that Nick was the main antagonist, that Jordan was actually only, at the moment, responding to the other man's aggression. But Nick's mood at the moment was such that he couldn't be reasoned with.

'So you do,' Nick said steadily. 'How long do you intend staying?'

Grace sensed Jordan's restrained glance in her direction, knowing Nick's rudeness was inexcusable, but also knowing that Jordan felt restricted, because of the company they were in, in his answers.

And as both men were guests in her home she felt responsible for what was happening, despite the fact that she knew both of them were perfectly capable of defending themselves, both verbally and physically.

'That, surely, is up to Jordan,' she attempted to gently rebuke Nick.

Challenging brown eyes met her eyes. 'Not necessarily,' Nick ground out.

Her cheeks became flushed. She allowed Nick a certain amount of familiarity in the running of the household, as she did Jessie too, knowing the two of them regarded Charlton House as their home and not just a boarding-house. But, even so, Nick was taking his position here a little too far.

She stood up to clear the plates, not caring that neither man had eaten anything; they had had their chance! 'And me,' she snapped. 'And, as far as I'm concerned, Jordan can stay here for as long as he wants to!'

She was usually very slow to anger, was more irritated than actually angry now, feeling the whole conversation to be unnecessary and hurtful.

'I haven't finished yet,' Jessie protested in a wounded voice as Grace would have automatically removed her plate too. Poor Jessie was only halfway through her meal, Grace realised. Really, these two men had her so unnerved that she didn't know what she was doing any more!

'Sorry, Jessie,' she said ruefully, replacing the plate, frowning her displeasure with Nick for creating this situation.

He stood up abruptly. 'I think I'll go up to my rooms,' he stated shortly.

Grace looked at him concernedly, knowing from the desolation in his eyes that he needed to get away from them all.

He hesitated at the door, looking back at Grace. 'You'll—come up later?'

She smiled gently, her irritation with him instantly gone. 'Yes.'

He nodded, leaving without another glance or word for anyone else in the room.

Timothy and Jessie knew better than to question Nick's moods, used to them by now, and Grace did her best to pretend she didn't notice Jordan's questioning looks as she moved quietly about the room.

She couldn't even begin to explain Nick's behaviour to the other man, was too close to it all herself to even attempt it.

The man was a bore, Jordan decided impatiently, *whoever* he was; he was still on edge from his conversation with the other man a good hour after the meal had finished and he sat in the comfort of the sitting-room with Jessie and Timothy, the latter supposedly studying the spellings he had been given for homework ready for a test later in the week.

Nick Parrish hadn't liked him before he even met him, that much was obvious to Jordan, although what he was supposed to have done to upset the other man he had no idea. Unless Nick

Parrish just didn't like the idea of a young man in the house, with his own interest in Grace.

Jordan felt more convinced than he had this morning that there was a special affection between the two; they had a way of communicating without the need of speech, an easy familiarity that came with emotional closeness for a long period of time.

Which rather put Jordan's own attraction to Grace in doubt. And he *was* attracted to her, to the point where he had actually thought of little else all day.

He had just enjoyed watching the movements of her hands and the tilting of her head during dinner, loved the slender delicacy of hands and face. The fantasies he had had of those hands caressing the nakedness of his body were just so incredible that he broke out in a cold sweat every time he thought of them!

She had disappeared into the kitchen again to clear away after the meal, refusing his offer of help, gently reminding him that, although she had appreciated his tidying away this morning after his breakfast, he was in fact a guest here, and so not expected to do it.

That had been an hour ago, and she still hadn't joined them in the sitting-room. He stood up restlessly, Jessie looking up from the knitting she was haphazardly doing; Jordan had already guessed, from what she had done so far, that it was a Balaclava for an elephant!

'I think I'll just take a stroll,' he excused lamely.

Jessie frowned. 'Outside? But it's very cold out there now, dear.'

'Er—no, I wasn't thinking of going outside,' he admitted ruefully.

The elderly lady nodded, smiling sweetly. 'Grace will be in her little sitting-room now,' she told him as if it was the most natural thing in the world to expect him to be looking for Grace.

Jordan gave her a sharp look, but there was such an expression of childish innocence on her face that he couldn't possibly read any hidden meaning into her words. 'Thank you,' he nodded abruptly, looking up to find Timothy grinning at him too; he scowled as he left the room with more haste than he would have wished.

Was his interest in Grace so obvious that even the slightly vague Jessie and a child could see it? It was ridiculous, made him feel utterly foolish, like a gauche schoolboy himself.

And yet he was drawn to that small sitting-room like a magnet, found himself knocking lightly on the door, entering after Grace had called out softly for him to do so. His breath caught in his throat as he looked across the room at her.

The lamp on the table was the only illumination, giving her hair the glow of burnished copper as it fell loosely down to the dark grey jumper she wore. Her skin had a peachy glow in the half-light too, her eyes a luminous grey.

And those eyes were gazing back at him curiously now as he stood tongue-tied just inside the doorway. He was thirty-two years old, for goodness' sake, not a raw teenager!

He closed the door firmly behind him, crossing the room to stand beside the big table she used as her desk. 'Bearing in mind what Nick said earlier——' he cleared his throat, his voice gruff '—I thought *you* might be wondering how long I intended staying on.' That hadn't been what he meant to say at all, he groaned inwardly, wishing he hadn't said it now as her face clouded over concernedly; the last thing he wanted to do was cause this woman any distress, for whatever reason.

She put down the pen she had been working with. 'I really should apologise for Nick's behaviour towards you earlier——'

'Why should you?' Jordan cut in lightly. 'He certainly doesn't intend to!'

Grace gave an answering rueful smile. 'No,' she acknowledged with a sigh. 'Nick very rarely apologises for anything.'

Jordan perched on the side of the table. 'I had already guessed as much,' he shrugged. 'I won't ask what his problem is, because I wouldn't ask you to break a confidence. Don't give the situation another thought,' he dismissed. 'Parrish and I are both big enough to take care of ourselves. At least,' he grimaced, 'we should be!' He stood up again, finding her closeness unsettling, moving restlessly about the room.

'Jordan...?'

Looking at her was his undoing, into those gentle grey eyes that seemed to see so much, to see the pain deep inside of him, holding his gaze now with questioning compassion as she stood up to cross the room to his side.

'Jordan, what's wrong?' she prompted softly.

His mouth twisted. 'Is it that obvious that something is?'

'I could lie and say no,' she said softly. 'But it *would* be a lie. At least, as far as I'm concerned.'

And this young lady rarely lied, he would guess. And if his disturbed emotional state was so obvious it was no wonder Jessie and Timothy had guessed he was, unknowing at the time, going off in search of Grace; everyone else in this household seemed to go to her when they were troubled or in pain—it had seemed the most natural thing in the world to Jessie and Timothy that he should do so too.

But that was a very good reason why he shouldn't burden her with his problems. Who did *she* go to when she was troubled? Parrish seemed the obvious answer to that question, and Jordan found he didn't like the idea of that at all.

'Come and sit down and talk to me.' Grace misread his sudden frown for anguish, her hand on his arm as they moved to sit on the sofa together.

Talk to her, she said, and yet he had never actually tried to put any of this into words before, not finding it easy to talk on a personal level to anyone at the best of times.

But Grace, with her warm grey eyes and gentle smile, was somehow different... He drew in a ragged breath. 'Two years ago, by the merest chance, I discovered that the man whom I had always believed to be my father wasn't my father at all!' It all came tumbling out in a rush, his voice edged with the pain of the revelation.

'Oh, Jordan——' tears welled up compassionately in Grace's eyes, her hand reaching out to clasp his '—what a shock for you!' That didn't even begin to describe how he had felt on learning the truth of his birth! 'But Timothy says you have a sister.' Grace frowned at the recollection. 'Is she... too?'

'No.' He gave a strained smile at Grace's awkwardness with the question, not least, he would guess, because Timothy must have gossiped that piece of information to her. 'Rhea is definitely legitimate. Although, ironically, she now bears the surname that should be mine,' he grimaced. 'You see, two years ago, she married my half-brother.'

It was no great wonder that Grace looked stunned; he had been numbed with shock himself for months after learning the truth!

It was an incredible story, and if Rhea hadn't met Raff Quinlan then Jordan would probably have lived the rest of his life never knowing that his father had, in fact, been Donald Quinlan and not James Somerville-Smythe.

Rhea had, quite literally, almost been run down by Raff one night, the latter insisting on taking her back to his home once it had been professionally established that she definitely hadn't sustained any injuries. Jordan and Rhea had been at odds with each other at the time, Rhea trying to convince the trustees of their father's will that she was responsible enough to take charge of her own inheritance when she reached twenty-one in a couple of months' time.

The long and the short of it was that, after starting out as antagonists, Rhea and Raff had fallen in love with each other. Jordan had liked the other man instantly, approving the match, finding himself very quickly introduced to the rest of the Quinlan family once Rhea and Raff had decided they were getting married. It had been a momentous meeting for all of them, Raff's aunt so stunned to realise who Rhea was, and consequently Jordan himself, that she had revealed the truth of his birth.

Years before, Jordan's mother, Diana, had been Raff's nanny. Raff's parents had been separated at the time, intending to divorce, and Diana and Donald had fallen in love, intending to marry themselves once Donald's divorce from

Helen was final. And then Raff's mother had been seriously injured in an accident, left paralysed, confined to a wheelchair, and Donald had been left with the intolerable choice of caring for the woman who was the mother of his son and actually still his wife, if only in name, or divorcing her regardless and marrying Diana, the woman he really loved.

It had been an impossible situation for all of them, and Diana had eventually been the one to make the decision, leaving Quinlan House without telling Donald she was going. Only Donald's sister had known Diana carried his child, that she chose to go rather than force him to make a decision that he could blame her and the child for, for the rest of his life.

Extraordinarily, Diana had met James Somerville-Smythe, a man already middle-aged, unable, or so he believed, to father a child of his own. And so Diana's predicament had seemed ideal to him. Diana, knowing she could never be with Donald, had decided to do the best that she could for her unborn child—had married the wealthy businessman, and Jordan had been brought up as James's son. Miraculously, eight years later, Diana and James had a child of their own, but Rhea's birth had robbed Diana of her own life, a fact James never quite forgave Rhea for. It was ironic, really; James had been determined that Jordan, who was no longer his legitimate heir, should inherit and run his business empire, while most of the time ignoring Rhea's very existence.

So, who was he—Jordan Somerville-Smythe or Jordan Quinlan? At the moment he just didn't know.

And Grace believed he was Jordan *Gregory*, he realised with a groan. And he couldn't tell her any of this, he also realised—not without revealing who he really was and promptly being asked to leave! It wasn't even possible to tell her Raff's surname; he was listed as the other director, along with Jordan Somerville-Smythe, of the company that wanted to buy this house!

He straightened. 'Forget I said any of this,' he dismissed lightly. 'You have enough worries of your own without listening to my problems too.'

'Oh, but——'

'You shouldn't be such a good listener,' he chided teasingly, tapping her playfully on the tip of her nose, realising, even as he did it, that the action must seem condescending.

She looked up at him with reproachful eyes, and he knew he had hurt her feelings. But he was hurting himself more, if she could only but know it; he would like nothing more than to pour his heart out to this hauntingly lovely young woman. Her lips were soft and pink, slightly parted, and he moved towards her as if drawn to a magnet.

* * *

Grace knew he was going to kiss her seconds before his mouth claimed hers, parting her lips slightly even as she tilted her head towards his.

His lips were firm as they touched hers, moving gently, rhythmically, his arms enfolding her almost tenderly against the hardness of his body. Warmth spread through her body, making her tremble; her arms moved up about his neck as she increased the pressure of his mouth on hers, the trembling of her body becoming a tangible thing as one of his hands moved down her back, exploring the gentle contours there before moving lower and fitting the perfect curve of her body into his.

Gently he outlined the soft tremor of her lips with his tongue, seeking entrance, but not demanding it, groaning low in his throat as her lips parted in response.

He was gentle and yet strong, teaching her of a passion that, although it burned beneath the surface, he could control for both of them. But as his mouth hardened, his arms tightened about her, it was a passion he didn't seem to want to end any more than she did.

His hands moved over her restlessly, barely touching her breasts, and yet she quivered beneath the caress, feeling a leaping of her senses. Jordan raised his head with a shuddering groan, looking down into her dazed, passion-filled face. It wasn't that she had never been kissed before, Grace thought, only that she had never responded in quite this way before! What was it about this man that was so different? This man, of all people!

His smile was strained as he smoothed her hair back from her flushed cheeks. 'You shouldn't be so tempting to kiss, either,' he spoke gruffly, moving abruptly away from her. 'I think I had better go for that walk outside in the cold after all!'

Grace watched him go, that feeling she had had yesterday, of her life having changed irrevocably with this man's arrival here, even more forceful...

CHAPTER FIVE

'I KNOW, I know.' Nick held up his hands defensively as he opened his door to Grace's knock a short time later. 'I behaved disgracefully to the new guest,' he admitted without any sign of apology for having done so.

She had forgotten all about that because of what had happened later, couldn't even remember what had been said during dinner between the two men, had come up here to the sanctuary of Nick's rooms for a completely different reason!

But now that he mentioned it...

'Yes, you did behave disgracefully,' she agreed disapprovingly, strolling past him into the lounge, not surprised to see it was even more untidy than it had been earlier in the day. 'And without provocation, I might add.' She turned to him, frowning her displeasure.

Nick gave a grimace, closing the door. 'The man is a walking provocation! You might at least have warned me——'

'Of what?' Her frown deepened.

His look was scornful. 'Grace, the man doesn't belong here——'

'Neither do you,' she pointed out firmly. 'Your place is in London.'

Nick's mouth tightened. 'I choose to stay here,' he bit out.

'So, for the moment, does Jordan,' she reasoned with a shrug.

'Why?' His eyes were narrowed to dark brown slits. 'He's obviously wealthy, certainly isn't lacking in self-confidence,' Nick scorned, 'so what is he doing hiding out here?'

'Nick——'

'The man is up to something, Grace.' He paced the room. 'I can feel it!'

'What you can *feel* is your own prejudice!' she told him impatiently. 'Jordan has just as much right to stay here, if he wishes, as you do——'

'So you told me earlier,' he recalled bitterly.

'Nick,' she sighed, 'I'm sure you're right, and he does have his own reasons for choosing to come *here*, of all places,' she added placatingly as he looked unconvinced, knowing better than anyone why Jordan was likely to be here. 'But shouldn't we respect the privacy of those reasons?' she encouraged softly.

'I don't like him——'

'Well, I do!' She could feel the heat spreading up her cheeks as Nick looked at her searchingly for her vehemence, shaking her head wearily. 'The conversation is irrelevant anyway, Nick, because I have already agreed he can stay on here. And I have no intention of going back on that decision,' she added firmly as he would have interrupted.

'Even if his presence here proves disruptive to the general peace and harmony of the household?' Nick challenged harshly.

Jordan had already proved to be very disruptive to her own peace and harmony! Grace had never felt so disturbed and unsettled, filled with a nervous tension that was completely alien to her nature. But the thought of his leaving now—oh, God, what was happening to her?

'I'm sure you're exaggerating the effect of his being here, Nick, because of your own dislike of him,' she sighed.

'I know the type——'

'Jordan isn't a *type*!' she snapped, and then sighed frustratedly as Nick's gaze narrowed on her suspiciously. 'Look, would you mind if I don't stay up here this evening? I'm really too tired.'

Tired was the last thing she actually felt, but she knew if she stayed up here long enough Nick would keep on and on at her until he discovered just how much she *didn't* dislike Jordan. And if he did that she would never hear the end of it!

'Not at all,' he snapped coldly, his displeasure obvious. 'I'm not in the mood tonight anyway.'

He was really very angry with her, she could tell that, and the last thing she wanted was to fall out with Nick; they had been together too long, shared too much pain and suffering. But the time she had spent in Jordan's arms earlier had thrown her into complete confusion, and she could see there was going to be no sympathy from Nick tonight in helping her understand that confusion.

Maybe Timothy's young innocence would offer more comfort...

She came to an abrupt halt in the doorway of her little brother's bedroom as she saw he wasn't alone, that seated on the side of his bed, reading him one of the adventure stories he liked so much, was Jordan!

Jordan had his back towards her as she came quietly into the room, and so he didn't see her, but Timothy did, and she raised a silencing finger to her lips so that he shouldn't alert Jordan to her presence and thus have his story interrupted.

She stood silently at the back of the bedroom, listening to the deep tenor of Jordan's voice rather than the story itself, watching him in profile, the normally harsh lines of his face softened to indulgence as he read to the rapt Timothy. Grace could easily understand her brother's fascination; Jordan told the story well, using all the differing voices to make it more interesting.

'I think perhaps you had better try to go to sleep now,' Jordan told the little boy ruefully when he came to the end of the story five minutes later.

'I think perhaps he had better try to go to sleep, too,' Grace remarked teasingly from behind him.

Jordan spun around guiltily, standing up, the book still in his hand. 'I was passing Tim's bedroom earlier, and——'

'You don't have to make excuses to me,' she laughingly replied as she moved towards them both. 'I know only too well how enticing this young man can be.' She ruffled Timothy's hair affectionately as he grinned up at her.

'I haven't intruded on something you usually do with Tim, have I?' Jordan looked deeply troubled at the thought.

And Grace could guess why, in part, from the little he had confided in her earlier. She knew there was a lot he hadn't told her, but it had been enough for her to realise how difficult he would find it to be accepted as part of any family now that he was very aware of the childhood he had lost with his own brother, and would hate to feel he was intruding now upon the relationship between Grace and her young brother.

'Not in the least,' she easily—and truthfully—dismissed that idea. 'If I have time I read Tim a story, but more often than not it just doesn't happen. I'm sure he's grateful you came along when you did. Besides,' she added teasingly, as he still didn't look convinced, 'you read so much better than I do!'

Jordan relaxed slightly, although he looked a little embarrassed that she had overheard him telling the story. 'I had plenty of practice with my sister Rhea,' he said, shrugging off that explanation.

He couldn't have been that old himself when his sister was old enough to enjoy having stories read to her; so where had his parents been?

There was so much she wanted to know about this man still, but until he chose to tell her—if he chose to tell her!—she couldn't force the issue. She was sure, having come to know him as little as she did, that he had already told her more about himself than he would have most people on so short an acquaintance. On any acquaintance! He was a solitary man, she felt sure of it.

'Sleep, young man.' She ruffled Timothy's hair again, didn't think he would appreciate her bending down for the hug and kiss he usually gave her, not in front of this man he was rapidly becoming fond of—not very manly, Timothy would probably think.

Grace gave him an understanding smile, waiting while he thanked Jordan for the story, and closing the door softly behind the two of them on their way out. She suddenly felt very self-conscious now they were alone in the hallway.

'He may protest a little, but he'll be asleep in minutes,' she told Jordan with certainty.

He looked down at her with dark eyes. 'Have you looked after him very long yourself?' His voice was gently enquiring.

'My mother died of complications at his birth,' she confirmed, her voice lowered too, so that Timothy shouldn't hear.

'My God!' He swallowed hard. 'So did mine. At Rhea's birth, I mean,' he explained a little agitatedly.

What a terrible thing for them to have in common. How terribly, terribly sad for all of them...

Grace put her hand on Jordan's arm. 'That must have been awful for you, given the other—circumstances,' she added awkwardly.

'Oh, I didn't know about any of that then.' He shook his head, giving a harsh, mirthless laugh. 'Thank God!'

But it gave them a bond.

She broke his gaze with effort, feeling herself being drawn further and further into whatever spell was being cast over the two of them. Not this man, she tried to warn herself. She couldn't become involved with this man, not emotionally or any other way.

'I'd better go down and pack Tim's lunch for tomorrow.' She turned away.

'Er——'

She turned back with a frown at the uncertainty in his voice; it was so unlike him that she couldn't help but give him her full attention.

Jordan looked a little embarrassed, another emotion that was alien to him, Grace was sure. 'I—would it be all right if I drove Tim to school in the morning? I—half promised him that I would. If you had no objections.' He grimaced.

Grace frowned up at him for several seconds while she took in exactly what he was asking, and then her lips began to twitch, and finally she couldn't stop the laughter. 'You've been had, Jordan,' she chuckled. 'You do realise that?' She shook her head ruefully. 'Today Tim went to school and boasted to all his friends about "being in a Jag"; tomorrow he intends to actually turn up in it!'

Jordan relaxed, grinning too. 'I guessed it was something like that,' he nodded ruefully.

'But you want to do it anyway?' she realised softly.

He looked a little anxious at the sudden disappearance of her humour. 'Only if you agree that I can. I wouldn't want to——'

'Jordan, Tim has too little contact with men as it is,' she cut in gently. 'I certainly wouldn't want to stop your driving him to school if that's what you want to do. Nick does his best, but—well, he has his own ghosts to deal with,' she dismissed abruptly. 'He does what he can,' she insisted firmly.

The uncertainty had disappeared from Jordan's face at the mention of the other man's name, and now he looked more like the distantly forbidding stranger she had first met yesterday. What was it about Nick that antagonised him so much?

Nick could be a little unorthodox in his way, she had to admit, but his heart was in the right place; he just didn't always know how to express what he was feeling.

Although neither he nor Jordan seemed to have had any problem in that direction earlier!

Damn Nick Parrish! Jordan inwardly cursed the other man. Why was the other man living here at all? What was he to Grace?

It was a sure fact that Parrish didn't belong in this gentle atmosphere any more than he did. Now that he had spoken to the other man he recognised the type only too well. There were dozens just like him in London—brash to the point of rudeness, cynical after years of mixing with a crowd where anything went, literally. Jordan despised the type, had never had time for any of them when he spent most of his time in town, so perhaps that was the reason Parrish had seemed so familiar the first time he had seen him.

And, whatever his reasons for being here, Jordan didn't like the thought of the other man being anywhere near Grace.

But he realised, despite the fact that Grace hadn't repulsed his kiss earlier, that he had no right to tell her how he felt about Nick. He felt hopeful at her response to him, knew she would never have let him kiss her, let alone responded to him the way she had, if she were involved with Parrish. So what was the relationship?

Timothy would know...

He despised himself now, for even thinking of stooping to such a level!

But the temptation was there, none the less...

'Let me make you a coffee while you pack Tim's lunch,' he found himself offering, whether as an apology for even having such underhand thoughts, or because he just didn't want to say goodnight to this beautiful woman just yet, he wasn't sure. A little of both, he suspected.

'I should say no.' Grace gave a regretful smile. 'After all, you are the guest here. But, to be truthful,' she added conspiratorially, 'the thought of someone making me a cup of coffee is a luxury that makes me feel thoroughly spoiled!' Her eyes glowed with the unexpected pleasure of it.

How easily pleased this young woman was, Jordan thought, once again held captive by her beauty, following her down the stairs, slightly regretful at leaving the intimacy of the dimly lit hallway, although the cosy comfort of the well-scrubbed kitchen more than made up for any disappointment he might feel.

As he made the coffee and Grace moved easily about the room preparing the lunch-box, he realised they might almost be any young couple enjoying the easy intimacy of a quiet evening together.

Incredible! He had never before had such disturbing thoughts. Disturbing to his enjoyed solitude, that was.

But did he actually enjoy that solitude any more, or was it just a comfortable cloak he draped about himself whenever he felt the need? Had seeing Rhea and Raff together the last couple of years made him hunger for the intimacy they had, the intimacy of a loving relationship?

God, *that* wasn't the 'something' he had been aching for—was it?

Because when he was with Grace that ache wasn't there any more...

CHAPTER SIX

'OH, TIMOTHY, we can't,' Grace protested wearily. 'It's far too early.'

'It's the first of December,' he pointed out hopefully, grey eyes raised in silent pleading.

They couldn't possibly put their Christmas decorations up yet; it was far too——

She had looked up and seen the same silent pleading in cobalt-blue eyes, Jordan having picked Timothy up from school a short time ago, the three of them now enjoying a warming drink together in the kitchen.

Over the last few days Jordan had been very helpful where Timothy was concerned, and as the two of them got on so well Grace could hardly object to the amount of time they spent together. She was a little concerned, however, about how Timothy was going to feel when it came time for Jordan to leave...

Although she had to admit she had started to put off that thought herself, Jordan having become so much a part of the household over the last four days.

That look of pleading, part of a conspiracy between the two, she was sure, over the Christmas decorations, was her undoing!

'We'll be the only people in the area with decorations and lights up,' she grumbled unconvincingly, already trying to remember where she had packed the decorations away when they had taken them down the previous year. After weeks and weeks of having the house cluttered up with them—or so it had seemed at the time!—she had just been glad to get them down out of the way. Besides, last Christmas had been their first since—— It hadn't been a happy time, although they had all tried, for Timothy's sake. To a child a week could seem a long time, and it had been six months since their father died—aeons to a small child. This year would be better, Grace was sure.

Would Jordan still be here at Christmas? It was over three weeks away; he had certainly given no indication that he would be staying as long as that. Although he had been out and bought another new jumper and a pair of trousers yesterday...

'That means she's given in—that we can!' Timothy was jumping up and down excitedly now, his eyes glowing. 'Can we do it now, Grace?' he urged eagerly. 'Can we? Oh, please——'

'After dinner, when we can all join in,' she cut in firmly, acknowledging that she had 'given in'. 'Christmas decorations are for the whole family.' She blushed slightly as dark blue eyes met her gaze steadily.

Timothy looked disappointed, but he quickly brightened again. 'Well, then, can Jordan and I get the things out ready?'

Jordan and I. Almost as if the two of them were on a level. And perhaps to Timothy they were, Grace realised ruefully.

'Homework first if you're going to spend the evening putting up decorations——'

'Oh, Grace, no!' her younger brother complained disgruntledly.

'Grace is right, Tim,' Jordan put in softly. 'This way you can enjoy the evening.'

Grace watched the emotions flickering across Timothy's face as the excitement of looking for the Christmas decorations and yet the desire to also please his new hero warred within him. The latter finally won as Timothy picked up his schoolbag before slowly going up to his room to do the homework.

The silence he left behind him was one of slight awkwardness.

'I shouldn't have interfered.' Jordan was finally the one to speak, grimacing as he did so.

'Of course you should,' Grace dismissed in some surprise. 'I don't mean interfered——' she felt warmth in her cheeks '—because I don't consider that was what you did. Timothy respects you, listens to you.'

Jordan was slightly pale, the new jumper he had bought and was wearing the same dark cobalt-blue of his eyes. His hair curled slightly

over its polo-neck, looking very dark. 'I'm intruding,' he muttered harshly.

She acted on impulse, moving to where he still
sat at the kitchen table to bend down and lightly
kiss him on the cheek. '*You* are far too sensitive,'
she teased him lightly. 'I'm really not the type of
woman to get in a possessive froth because
someone else chooses to help discipline Timothy.
I just want him to grow up respecting his elders.
And I believe he already does that,' she shrugged.

A nerve pulsed in Jordan's cheek where she
had just kissed him. 'I've been accused of being
*in*sensitive.'

She made a face. 'Only by people who don't
really know you, I'm sure.'

His mouth twisted. 'They seem to think they
do!'

'Well, we know better. Timothy and I,' she explained at his questioning look.

He stood up slowly, suddenly very close. 'You
don't really know me at all,' he told her huskily.

'What I do know, I like. And I trust Timothy's
judgement,' she added firmly, aware of the faint
noises of the other people in the house, and yet
feeling very much alone down here with Jordan,
almost as if they were in a world apart from
everyone else.

Jordan shook his head. 'He could be wrong
about me too.'

Grace met his gaze unblinkingly. 'I don't think
so.' She spoke huskily as he moved even nearer.

'Don't say I didn't try to warn you,' he groaned, his arms going about her waist as he stepped in close to her body.

There was so much strength in his wide shoulders, tapered waist and powerful thighs, his legs long and muscular beneath dark trousers, and yet he didn't try to use any of it on her.

He didn't have to! She swayed towards him, her eyes closed.

'Grace...?'

She blinked up at him, just wanting him to kiss her as he had before.

'Don't say I didn't warn you!' he repeated forcefully, his head lowering to hers.

There was no tentative exploration this time, lips possessing, bodies welded together, hers somehow fitting perfectly along the lean length of Jordan's, her arms up about his neck as her fingers became entangled in the dark thickness of his hair.

She was even starting to love the smell of him, a clean, muscular smell with the faint tang of aftershave that was only Jordan!

Their lips moved together hungrily, warm breath scalding her cheeks as Jordan trailed kisses down her throat to the pulse that beat at its hollow base. Pleasure coursed through her body as a fiery tongue caressed that hollow, sending shivers of sensation down her spine and arms to her very fingertips.

She gasped as his hand moved to cup her breast, but her gasp quickly turned to a groan as a single caress sought the hardened tip, the heat in her body becoming a blaze now, her fingers in his hair roughly pulling him to her as his lips returned to hers.

But suddenly she was no longer in his arms but standing alone, her hand reaching out to grasp the table in case she should sway and fall, staring at him in numbed surprise at his sudden desertion of her. Was this what he had been warning her about? What had happened to make him——?

'Well, well, isn't this cosy?' drawled an all-too-familiar voice from behind her.

Grace spun round almost guiltily to look at Nick, whose blond brows were raised tauntingly in his cynical face, then turned slowly back to look at Jordan as he stood so tautly across the room, knowing he must have heard the approach of Nick's footsteps down the stairs and moved away so suddenly to save her embarrassment with the other man.

Thank God he had; Nick would have demanded an explanation if he had actually found them in each other's arms! And even she wasn't sure what was happening between herself and Jordan, certainly couldn't explain the attraction to Nick.

He was looking at the two of them slightly suspiciously anyway, as if he half guessed what had taken place in this room minutes ago.

Which wasn't altogether surprising; Jordan's usually immaculate hair was still ruffled by her fingers, and she was sure she hadn't escaped unscathed herself, her hair in more disarray than usual, her lips feeling swollen from the kisses they had shared. She knew Nick wouldn't miss such obvious signs of intimacy. Which was unfortunate, because in his unnecessary guise as protector to her he was sure to be even more brittle and sarcastic with Jordan than he usually was.

She looked at Jordan pleadingly, willing him not to react. But it would be too much to hope that he wouldn't; the two men were too much alike!

'We were just discussing Christmas decorations,' she spoke in a voice she knew was far too loud!

Nick adopted a challenging pose as he leaned back against one of the kitchen units, his arms folded across the chest of the thick shirt he wore tucked into worn denims. 'Oh, yes?'

Her mouth firmed at the taunt in his voice. 'Timothy wants to put them up this evening.'

'And?'

She felt the colour enter her cheeks. 'And so we're putting them up this evening,' she admitted ruefully.

'I thought we might be,' Nick drawled derisively.

'Timothy is just excited about the prospect of Christmas,' Jordan put in defensively.

Brown eyes flashed angrily at the rebuke. 'I haven't forgotten what it's like to be a child at Christmas, Gregory,' Nick growled.

Jordan stiffened, glancing at Grace, as if he half expected—— No, he couldn't think she would have confided any of the things he had told her about his private life to Nick!

'Nick believes I over-indulge Timothy,' she hastened to explain Nick's attitude.

'Timothy is a well-balanced little boy,' Jordan instantly defended. 'Certainly not spoiled.'

Oh, dear, she had introduced yet another volatile subject between these two men. Was there one that wasn't?

'I——'

'To get back to the subject of the decorations,' she firmly cut into what she knew was going to be Nick's angry reply. 'We'll need them to be brought down from one of the bedrooms.'

'I'll get them, I know where they are—after all, I helped put them away last year,' Nick answered her, but he was looking at Jordan with narrowed eyes. 'It seems a pity that you'll be helping to put up the Christmas decorations but won't actually be here then,' he added challengingly.

The next remark was predictable in the face of Nick's deliberate baiting of the other man!

'I have no plans to leave before that time,' was Jordan's instant come-back.

Anger flared in Nick's eyes, and, although it had been slow in coming, Grace thought he might finally be beginning to realise he had met a man who was more than a match for him. He made no answering comment anyway, leaving abruptly to go in search of the decorations!

Arrogant bastard!

Jordan watched the other man leave the room with narrowed eyes, wishing his personal assistant would hurry up and find that file on Charlton House and its occupants, wanting to know more about Nick Parrish, feeling out of his depth with him without that detailed information. He should have read the damned thing more thoroughly when it was originally on his desk!

And now, it seemed, he had been antagonised into committing himself to staying on here for Christmas. Three and a half weeks away...

The situation with Grace was getting beyond his control already; God knew what would happen after another month in the same house as her!

And Rhea and Raff would be expecting him back at Quinlan House for Christmas; in fact they were counting on it—they always spent Christmas together.

Besides, he couldn't continue to ignore his business commitments indefinitely. Much as the temptation was to do just that.

That realisation stopped him in his tracks. He had never felt that way about his work before; it had always come first with him . . .

'Jordan?'

He turned to Grace, forcing a reassuring smile as she looked at him anxiously. Whatever his problems, this enchantingly lovely woman, both inside and out, was not one of them. His growing feelings for her were, but Grace herself was not . . .

'Miles away,' he excused, quite truthfully as it happened; Hampshire, and Rhea and Raff, *were* miles away. It might be better if they weren't. 'Do you think I could——?'

'Ah, here the two of you are.' Jessie smiled at the pair of them glowingly as she entered the kitchen. 'Jordan, there's a telephone call for you.'

He could feel himself growing pale. 'For me?' he echoed hollowly. It couldn't be. No one knew—Rhea . . . ?

It had been too much to hope that his little sister would meekly accept his decision to take a breal here without trying to make further contact with him; he should have known her better than that, Jordan realised.

But she could have ruined everything for him, blundering in the way she had!

That realisation made him aware of just how emotionally involved with Grace he was becoming, of how reluctant he was to have the gentle trust in her eyes when she looked at him turn to disgust and suspicion. As it surely must, even if the reasons for his assuming the identity of J. Gregory were completely innocent, his original reasons for coming to Charlton House all but forgotten—certainly they had been dismissed. Grace, and the other people who lived in this exceptional house, should be left to enjoy living here in peace and harmony.

Although, in the circumstances, Grace was hardly likely to believe he felt that way, would hate his subterfuge, being so lacking in it herself.

'Oh, yes,' Jessie confirmed lightly. 'It's a young lady,' she added coyly.

Definitely Rhea, because there was no other 'young lady' in his life. Damn! How was he going to explain any of this to Grace?

'Jordan?' Grace prompted now in a puzzled voice as he still made no effort to go upstairs and take his call.

'Oh, yes,' he acknowledged with a feeling of dread; Jessie was sure to blurt out the truth of his identity—even though she perhaps didn't realise the enormity of it!—while he was upstairs talking to Rhea! And Grace would know exactly what she thought of it—and him! 'I—shouldn't be long,' he added lamely, reluctant to leave the two women alone, but knowing he had no choice.

He would have time enough to attempt to defend his actions to Grace after he had spoken to Rhea, he realised dully.

Nick Parrish was clattering back down the stairs as Jordan approached them, and so he stood and waited for the other man to get to the bottom.

'Quite right,' he drawled mockingly. 'It's bad luck to cross on the stairs.'

Bad luck; Jordan felt as if his world was about to fall apart before he was completely sure what he was looking for!

'Changed your mind about the decorations?' the other man taunted, easily carrying the box of them, and assuming Jordan was going to his room.

They faced each other at the bottom of the stairs, obvious adversaries.

'I rarely change my mind once it's made up,' Jordan told the other man harshly. 'And I knew from the minute I met you that I wasn't going to like you; nothing that has happened since that time has changed that opinion!' With this parting shot he moved unhurriedly up the stairs.

He knew he had been provoked, after their earlier conversation, into declaring war on Nick, and yet the man seemed to take delight in being deliberately insulting. The same instant dislike Jordan had felt for him, he would say.

But he had much more important things to think about than Nick Parrish just now!

He picked up the telephone receiver from where
it lay on the table-top in Grace's office-cum-
sitting-room. 'Rhea?' he rasped without
preamble, absolutely furious at the trouble she
had undoubtedly caused for him here with her
unwanted telephone call.

'Mr Gregory, I presume?' she returned drily,
not at all deterred by his anger.

'What—how——?' He knew he was gabbling,
but for once, he admitted, Rhea had caught him
off guard.

His sister laughed softly. 'I've just had a rather
garbled   conversation   with   your   Miss
Brown——'

'Grace?' That startled him out of his confusion. Grace had been down in the kitchen with
him when the call had come through; he could
still remember the imprint of her body pressed
up against his so that not even a wisp of air separated them...so how could she possibly
have——? Jessie! Somehow Rhea had made the
same mistaken assumption he had when he'd first
arrived here. 'Oh, yes?' he prompted lightly;
there might be hope for him yet, Rhea had
mockingly called him 'Mr Gregory', after all!

'She sounds very sweet, Jordan,' Rhea acknowledged. 'But a little odd too.'

'She is very sweet,' he confirmed warily.

'Always the gentleman, Jordan,' Rhea teased.
'But, among all the confusion of our cross-
purpose conversation, I managed to ascertain

that the man I wanted to talk to was the new boarder, a Mr Gregory. Gregory?'

'It's a long story, Rhea,' he sighed, wishing he weren't having this conversation at all.

'I'm in no hurry,' she mocked.

'But I am!' He sat on the side of the desk. 'I'll explain everything when I get back.'

'And just when is that going to be?' she put in quickly.

'I'm not sure,' he dismissed easily. 'Do you happen to know if David has found the Charlton House file yet?'

'That's one of the reasons I telephoned there; none of us was absolutely sure where you were staying, and so David has no idea where to send the file. Or if you're still interested,' Rhea added curiously.

'I'm still interested,' he told her firmly. 'And now you know David can send the file here.'

'To Mr Gregory,' she guessed drily.

'To Mr Gregory,' he confirmed tautly. ' "One of the reasons you telephoned"?' he prompted abruptly.

She laughed softly at his astuteness. 'I also wanted to know how you were,' she admitted ruefully.

'And exactly where I was,' he guessed shrewdly. 'Well, now you know!'

'So I do,' Rhea teased unconcernedly. 'Feel any more inclined to tell me what you're up to?'

'No.'

She laughed softly. 'I thought not,' she drawled. 'Well, as long as you're sure you're all right...?'

'I'm a big boy now, Rhea,' he sighed, 'so stop worrying about me.'

'I can't do that, Jordan.' She was suddenly serious. 'I happen to love you.'

They weren't a sentimental family, their affection for each other just an accepted thing between them, and so his sister's declaration was all the more touching because of that.

'I love you too,' he told her gruffly. 'But don't telephone me here again!' he added hardly.

Rhea chuckled in delight at his instant switch back into character. 'No, sir. I must say, you sound happy enough,' she said curiously. 'The change is obviously as good as a rest in your case.'

'Rhea, you're starting to waffle yourself now,' he told her with his usual brutal honesty. 'Go away and pester your husband, or feed the baby, or something!'

'Raff is busy at the moment playing "mine host", and Diana is already in bed for the night,' his sister dismissed lightly.

'There's always "or something",' Jordan reminded her callously. 'Goodnight, Rhea.'

'Goodnight, Jordan,' she came back unconcernedly. 'Take care.'

All he could think of once he had replaced the receiver was that his real identity hadn't been revealed after all!

* * *

Grace didn't think she would ever tire of watching Timothy's face as the decorations went up, giving the rooms and hallways a glittering festivity, albeit a tarnished adornment that she knew the adults, at least, would be long tired of before Twelfth Night, when they officially had to all come down again!

But for the moment the faded rooms were taking on a light and colour that was mesmerisingly beautiful, and all of them seemed to be infected with the Christmas spirit.

Even Nick—who had decided to join them at the last minute—and Jordan seemed to have dropped hostilities for this special time! Although there had been one small dispute over where a particular shining star should be suspended from...

Timothy had ended that disagreement before it could actually become a proper one by putting it over the fireplace, so that none of them should forget that Christmas was actually about Jesus being born. Grace had ruefully recognised her own words being thrown back at them! But she was pleased to learn that Timothy had actually listened to her and understood what she had been trying to say to him.

She watched Jordan now as he stood on one of the step-ladders draping holly behind a mirror. Would he be with them for Christmas this year? He had said 'yes' earlier, although she realised that that had been after much provocation. She couldn't honestly see him staying on here that long.

'You're supposed to kiss each other,' Timothy giggled beside her.

Grace looked down at him a little dazedly, shaken by his remark after her thoughts had so recently been on Jordan; Timothy couldn't possibly know anything about the kisses they had shared both this morning and tonight, and yet what else could he——?

'Up here, Grace!' Jessie called teasingly, and Grace looked up to find the other woman on the other pair of step-ladders with a piece of mistletoe she was intending to attach to the ceiling with the aid of a drawing-pin.

As Grace was innocently standing next to Nick when the challenge was made, it was clear what the mischievous pair's intention was!

Jordan had turned to look at them all now, eyes narrowed, waiting to see what her next move would be. Grace hesitated because of that, but Nick felt no such qualms, sweeping her up into his arms to hug and kiss her.

'Your turn now, Jordan,' Timothy dared, his eyes aglow.

Jordan shook his head, coming down the ladder. 'I don't think that's the way it works, Tim,' he said ruefully.

'You have to get the girl you want to kiss actually next to you underneath the mistletoe,' Nick explained to the little boy, his arm still about Grace's shoulders.

'Well? Tim frowned pointedly at Jordan, as the latter didn't move.

'I don't think——' Jordan broke off, his gaze fixed somewhere behind Grace and Nick. 'Jessie, I think perhaps you ought to come down from there,' he advised in a calm voice, moving towards the elderly lady as he did so.

'Yes, I think you—oh!'

Before any of them could reach Jessie she had misplaced her foot on the next step, missing it completely as she tumbled down on to the carpeted floor with a telling thump.

CHAPTER SEVEN

GRACE hated hospitals, had done so ever since her mother had died, and then her father followed her eighteen months ago. For some people they could be a place of hope, of life reborn, but they had only ever held unhappiness for Grace and her family, and she hated being here now.

They were examining Jessie, the elderly lady clutching on to Grace's hand, the pain in her ankle the obvious cause of the trouble. Grace knew that boded ill. It hadn't been a very big fall, a couple of feet at most, but Jessie was old, her bones brittle, and Grace very much suspected she might have broken her ankle. It would be awful if she had.

Jordan had taken control of the situation after Jessie's fall, insisting she wasn't moved, instructing Nick to go and call an ambulance once he had seen just how much pain Jessie was in — too much really for her to just be bruised. Nick ordinarily wasn't a man who liked being given orders by anyone, but even he recognised the seriousness of the situation and went without demur to use the telephone.

Tim had been the one who worried Grace the most, ashen-faced, standing back across the room from them all.

Grace would have liked to go to him, to re-assure him, but Jessie was crying softly, ob-viously in shock as well as pain, and holding Grace's hand so tightly she felt as if the bones were crushed.

And Jessie had continued to hold her hand, had refused to let go even once the ambulance had arrived and the men with the vehicle had managed to get her outside on a stretcher and inside the ambulance.

There was no question but that Grace would accompany the elderly lady to the hospital, and yet she was still concerned about Tim, so she was grateful to Nick when he opted to stay behind with the little boy, while Jordan went with the two women in the ambulance.

Grace was grateful for his reassuring presence, for the way he had taken charge at the hospital, sitting outside in the waiting-room now.

Jessie wept anew when the doctor confirmed her ankle was broken and that they would have to admit her, and her bony fingers grasped Grace's hand as if she was frightened to let go in case she should never see Grace again.

Grace wanted to say something to comfort her, to reassure her, and yet the words stuck in her throat, words she had used twice in her life already—and they had proved to be lies. Neither

her mother nor father had ever left hospital again.

And then, miraculously, Jordan was there, talking softly to Jessie, comforting her in the way Grace couldn't, promising that they would stay with her while she was taken to the ward, that they wouldn't leave her until she was asleep—the doctor murmured that they were seeing about giving the elderly lady something to kill the pain and help her sleep right now—and that they would be back again in the morning; Jessie wouldn't even realise they had been away!

Grace felt ashamed that she wasn't able to give Jessie the support she needed, although for the moment, with Jordan's strength to draw from, it seemed to be enough for Jessie to have her hand to cling to while Jordan talked to her.

'She'll be fine,' Jordan reassured her in the taxi on the way back home.

But would she, *would she*? Jessie was as much a part of Grace's family as Timothy and Nick were, had become like an honorary grandmother to herself and Timothy. Charlton House was going to seem very empty without Jessie's happy presence.

'I should have made her get down from the ladder as soon as I saw her there,' Grace berated herself. 'I hadn't even realised she was up the ladder until——'

'Grace, self-condemnation, from any of us, isn't going to help anyone——' Jordan's hand stilled the nervous movements of hers '—least of all Jessie.'

Tears welled up in her eyes. 'I love her so much, I don't think I could bear it if——'

'Now that is just ridiculous,' he cut in briskly, unconcerned by the presence of the man driving the taxi as he slipped his arm about Grace's shoulders, nestling her snugly against him. 'Jessie is very healthy for her age——'

'But that's just it,' she choked, the tears starting to fall. 'Jessie is seventy-three, and——'

'As strong as an ox, despite her obvious look of frailty,' Jordan insisted firmly. 'She eats well, and is well looked after, and I see no reason why she shouldn't make a complete recovery from this.'

Grace looked at him searchingly in the dim lighting given off by the streetlamps before they reached the open countryside on the approach to the house. 'You aren't just saying that?'

His mouth twisted. 'Have I given you any reason to suppose I ever "just say" anything?' he said self-derisively.

Grace gave a tearful smile. 'No.'

'And I'm not about to start now,' he assured her decisively. 'Jessie needs *you* to be strong and positive now, so I recommend you get a good night's rest so that you feel able to cope with tomorrow.'

'Recommend?' she teased, feeling as if a weight was being lifted from her shoulders, but not

daring to question why she trusted Jordan enough
to accept it as being so when he told her everything was going to work out fine; she might be
too disturbed by the answer she might find!

'Order, then,' he acknowledged ruefully. 'But
my sister tells me I'm far too fond of giving
orders.' He grimaced. 'And expecting them to be
obeyed!'

'She sounds nice,' Grace said interestedly.

'I like her—but then, I daren't do otherwise!'
He chuckled softly.

'Tell me more about her,' she encouraged, sure
there wasn't a woman alive whom Jordan was
genuinely in awe of. 'She sounds a lot like you.'

He started to talk about Rhea, of her madcap
teenage years, the sense of fun she still had, although it was tempered slightly now by the responsibilities of marriage, her daughter, and by
the way she helped her husband run their business
on a day-to-day level.

Grace could hardly tell Jordan she would like
to meet his sister—that sounded a little too familiar in the circumstances—and yet Rhea was
only a couple of years older than herself, and she
sounded good fun. She *would* like to meet her.

She knew Jordan was talking now for the sake
of distracting her, but she liked listening to him,
enjoyed the sound of his voice, as she rested her
head drowsily against his shoulder, loving that
male smell of him.

By the time they reached the house she did feel in control again, with the conviction that, with their help, Jessie would get well again. She had to, they all needed her!

There was only a light on in the hallway downstairs when they let themselves in, and Grace guessed that both Nick and Tim would have gone to bed by now; it was very late, after all.

'I'll make you some coffee or a hot chocolate to help you——'

'I'll do that,' Nick interrupted Jordan's offer as he came noisily down the stairs. 'I think you had better go up to Tim, Grace,' he sighed. 'I've tried to reassure the little chap, but he seems convinced Jessie is going to die, and refused to even think about going to sleep until you got back from the hospital.'

'Oh, God.' Grace paled. 'I knew he was upset, but—I'll go up to him.'

'He's in my rooms,' Nick told her heavily.

'I'll go up with you,' Jordan instantly offered.

Grace turned to him, knowing it wasn't an offer at all, that Jordan intended coming upstairs with her whether she wanted him to or not.

But she wanted him to.

Jordan just wanted to hold her, to tell her everything was going to be all right, but he had known as he had held her in the taxi earlier that Grace didn't very often give in to her own feelings of emotional need, that she had carried the responsibilities of this house and her family for too long to be able to do that easily.

She was too young for all this, too young and lovely, and he wanted to protect her from any more distress.

He was shaken by the fierceness of his own emotions. He knew he cared for Grace, but was he actually falling in love with her?

The possibility of that shook him more than anything else ever had in his life—even the trauma he had experienced two years ago. What did he know about love, especially for a unique woman like Grace?

He followed her now as she went up to the top of the house, where Nick Parrish's rooms seemed to be; Tim was sitting up on the sofa in the sitting-room there, albeit covered with a blanket. The grey eyes so like Grace's were wide with fear, his face deathly white, and he stared silently at Grace as she entered the room, seeming afraid to speak.

Grace went straight to him, and sat on the edge of the sofa. 'She's all right, Tim,' she soothed calmly, her own earlier panic put firmly to one side as she concentrated on the distressed child. 'Her ankle is broken—but she's strong,' she added firmly as Tim gave a dismayed gasp, using Jordan's words as her own in an effort to comfort him. 'I'll take you in to see her tomorrow.'

He shook his head. 'I don't want to go.'

'Tim!' she gasped her dismay, turning to Jordan again for help.

'Tim, for Jessie's sake I think you should go in and see her.' Jordan stepped forward out of the shadows. 'She needs you,' he added as Tim would have protested again. 'How do you think you would feel if the positions were reversed and Jessie refused to come and see you in hospital?' he reasoned gently.

He could see the child was beginning to waver at this, obviously not liking that thought at all. 'Jessie is going to be very lonely in hospital until they allow her to come home again.' Jordan pressed home his point while he felt he had some chance of success.

'Yes, we have to be very strong for her,' Grace said, taking up his line of argument as she saw it was having some effect on Tim. 'Jessie can't do it all alone,' she added softly.

Tim still looked indecisive, although some of the colour had returned to his cheeks. 'I'm not getting the tree or decorating it until Jessie comes home,' he finally said stubbornly, but it was at least an indication that he now accepted the elderly lady *would* come back.

Jordan hoped, more than anything, that he wasn't wrong about that! Old and slightly scatty as Jessie was, this family loved and needed her, he could see that. Jessie couldn't know just how fortunate she was...

But his attention returned to Grace and Tim as the little boy began to look anxious again.

'Peter won't come and take Jessie away now, will he?' Tim frowned up at Grace.

Her eyes widened, and Jordan could see the suggestion was a shock to her. 'I hadn't thought of that...' she gasped.

'But will he?' Timothy persisted worriedly.

'Of course not,' Grace dismissed with a certainty Jordan could see she was far from feeling, by the sudden shadows in her eyes. 'Jessie belongs here with us,' she added determinedly—although the shadows still remained.

Who the hell was Peter? Why should he want to take Jessie away from here? What *right* did he have to do so?

Hell, he hated being this much in the dark about anything. If that file on Charlton House didn't turn up in the post on Saturday morning, at the latest, he was going to give David his notice!

There was still the puzzle of Nick Parrish to bother him. This room obviously bore the stamp of the other man's personality, an indication of how at home he was here. The kitchen area could be seen through an open doorway to the left, but there were two other doors firmly closed to prying eyes—and Jordan readily admitted his *were* prying. His growing feelings for Grace made it vitally important that he know just how important Nick Parrish was to Grace herself.

What lay behind those two closed doors? A bedroom behind one, of course, but the other one? As far as Jordan could tell the other man rarely left the house, certainly hadn't gone out to work on any of the days Jordan had been there. So what did he do with himself all day?

Saturday morning at the latest, or David was sacked!

It was no good to keep telling himself he should have taken more notice of the Charlton House file himself in the first place instead of just treating it like another business proposal. He hadn't, and he knew that part of the reason for that was his growing dissatisfaction with his life, business as well as personal. And so to all intents and purposes he had arrived here completely unprepared, floundering about in the dark, too proud to ask David or Rhea to read out the relevant details over the telephone to him; God knew what Rhea would make of that if he did!

But he would find out about Nick Parrish; it was becoming vitally important to his peace of mind that he did so!

'Hot chocolate all round,' the man in question announced lightly as he came into the room bearing a tray containing four mugs.

Timothy blossomed in the reassuring presence of the three adults, brightening considerably as they all sat and drank their chocolate. This was obviously a treat for him, and one, now that he was less upset, he took full advantage of.

'Bed,' Grace finally told him firmly as he did his best to keep his eyes open.

His eyes instantly widened in an effort not to look tired. 'I'm not going to be ready for bed for ages yet——'

'You're going to bed now, young man,' he was told firmly by his sister. 'I'll take you to your room now, and then I have to make a telephone call. Peter,' she murmured softly to Nick as he looked at her frowningly for the lateness of the call, while Timothy was busy collecting up his things now that it seemed he wasn't about to get away with staying up any later.

The other man's frown didn't lighten at this brief explanation. 'Jordan and I can put Tim to bed,' Nick told her firmly. 'You go and make your call.'

Grace stood up, laying a gentle hand against Timothy's cheek. 'That all right with you?'

'Oh, yes,' he grinned at her as Nick picked him up and threw him over his shoulder.

Considering the other man's previous antagonism, Jordan couldn't help but admit to feeling surprised at his inclusion of him now, but he followed the man and boy unquestioningly down to Timothy's bedroom.

Nick had managed to get Timothy into his pyjamas earlier, but Tim had obviously stubbornly held out against anything else. The other man put the giggling little boy down in the bed now before turning to Jordan. 'Tim tells me you read a mean bedtime story.'

'Oh, yes, Jordan——' Timothy clapped his hands together in approval of this suggestion '—please!'

Jordan was still taken aback by the other man's sudden friendliness, he had to admit. From resenting him without even giving him a chance, the other man now seemed to have accepted him. Nick Parrish was an enigma!

'A short one,' Nick told Timothy now. 'You have school in the morning.'

Jordan gave a rueful shrug. 'I think he's going to have to give school a miss tomorrow.'

'Hurray!' Timothy squealed excitedly.

Nick gave Jordan a conspiratorial smile. 'I think you could be right,' he nodded.

Jordan didn't have any more time to ponder Nick's change of attitude, although he wasn't surprised to see, for all the boy's claims to the contrary, that Tim fell asleep after only three pages of the wanted story. He quietly closed the book, looking down at the youthfully vulnerable face, so like Grace's; he just wanted to hug the little boy.

'Endearing little devil, isn't he?'

Jordan looked up with a start, having briefly forgotten Nick Parrish was still in the bedroom with them. He stood up abruptly. 'Yes—yes, he is,' he nodded curtly.

The two men eyed each other awkwardly once outside the bedroom.

'Look,' Nick finally began slowly, 'I think I might have been a little—unwelcoming, when you first arrived here.' His voice was gruff. 'I—but you were there tonight, for Jessie, and for Grace, when they needed you, and so—well——' he struggled to find the right words '—welcome to Charlton House!' He held his hand out to shake Jordan's.

Jordan returned the gesture a little dazedly; this was the last thing he had been expecting.

Great; now he had been put in a position where he felt a certain responsibility of friendship towards the other man. That was the last thing he needed, feeling as he did himself about Grace!

Nick grimaced. 'I can tell you now that there's going to be trouble from Peter Amery. Jessie's son,' he explained at Jordan's questioning look. 'We had better go down and see how Grace got on with her call to him,' he sighed, obviously expecting the outcome to be a bad one.

Jessie's *son*! And he sounded as if he was going to be a complication. But no more so, surely, than the sudden friendliness of the man Jordan considered to be his rival where Grace was concerned!

Grace sat behind her desk in the little sitting-room, heard the two men come down the stairs together, and their approach to the sitting-room now. She blinked up at them a little dazedly, having received another blow she hadn't even considered earlier.

She had told Peter, Jessie's son, the situation, and was sure from his reaction to the news that he was going to use this situation to try to force the issue of having Jessie put into a home.

Most sons would have just been concerned that their mother was all right, the relief of that superseding everything else. But not Peter Amery—he would use this situation to his advantage if he could; Grace had no doubt of that.

In fact, he had just implied as much, had told her he would be going to see his mother in the morning, and that he would assess the situation then. Grace knew exactly what he meant by 'assess the situation'!

She had had a long-running battle with Peter Amery about his mother. He wanted Jessie put into a home, where he wouldn't have to give her another thought if he didn't want to. Jessie wanted to maintain her independence for as long as she could, to stay here at Charlton House, where she felt so much at home, with the people she loved; Grace knew that.

The accident, with Peter Amery's implication that there had been a lack of caring for Jessie's welfare for it to have happened at all, could jeopardise all that. And possibly now he would have the power to insist upon it.

Grace stood up abruptly. 'I think battle over Jessie is about to commence,' she choked, the tears finally beginning to fall in earnest.

And she didn't realise, for some time afterwards, that it was to the reassurance of Jordan's arms that she moved...

CHAPTER EIGHT

GRACE stared at the woman who stood on the doorstep, completely tongue-tied for once in her life, having answered the ringing of the doorbell in all innocence a couple of minutes ago.

Was this Charlton House? the young woman had frowned. When Grace had confirmed it was, she had then asked if she might see Jordan!

His wife?

The woman was certainly lovely enough, deep-red hair almost down to her waist, although the burnished waves were secured back at the moment in a single plait down the length of her spine, her face small and pointed, dominated by dark blue eyes.

Jordan's wife? Grace wondered again. Who else would come all the way up here, hundreds of miles away from his home, to look for him?

Jordan's wife, Grace realised with a sinking heart; it had to be.

When, last night, he had kissed *her* with passion and need. Not just earlier in the kitchen, but later on in her bedroom too.

She had felt so tired and defeated after her call to Peter Amery and then her fit of weeping, had raised no objections when between them Nick and

Jordan had decided she needed to get to bed and have some sleep.

She had been too weary to even notice the new-found truce that seemed to exist between the two men, had only realised that this morning when Nick joined them downstairs in the kitchen for breakfast and the two men had actually shared *The Times* newspaper that had been delivered, Jordan taking the business section, Nick the other part!

But last night she had been too tired to notice any of that, going along meekly with Jordan when he insisted on accompanying her to her bedroom—she should have realised then that something had happened to change things between the two men; Nick wouldn't normally have let any man go to her bedroom with her. Not without a fight!

Grace had been surprised at how exhausted she had felt once she got to her bedroom—almost too weary to bother to get undressed.

Jordan had been the one to remove her clothes, item by item, with infinite gentleness, until he had slipped her silky nightgown over her head, and turned back the bedclothes before tucking her comfortably beneath them.

Grace had been the one to reach up and entwine her arms about his neck, pulling him down to her, groaning low in her throat as his lips gently claimed hers.

But gentleness wasn't what either of them wanted, and desire had quickly raged out of control; Grace's nightgown was soon discarded again, and Jordan's lips trailed moistly down her body to capture one turgid peak, caressing the hardened nub with the heat of his tongue.

She had wanted him so badly at that moment, arching up against him, seeking further contact, needing——

'I can't make love to you now!' Jordan had pulled back, breathing heavily, a slight flush to the hardness of his cheeks. 'Not now, Grace,' he groaned. 'It isn't that I don't want to——' he looked pained at the bewilderment in her face '—but when I make love to you I want it to be with no shadows hanging over us. Grace, do you understand?'

She had understood, but it hadn't stopped her longing for him; her body had ached for hours after he had left her, only the fact that he had said 'when' and not 'if' he made love to her stopping her from going to his bedroom.

And now, the very next afternoon, his wife had turned up here looking for him!

She looked nice too, her eyes warm, her smile friendly, her expression completely unsuspecting, full of bright enquiry. And Grace was the one left feeling guilty—when she had responded out of complete innocence!

'Is Jordan here?' The woman's smile began to falter. 'I do have the right house, don't I?'

'Oh, you have the right house,' Grace confirmed huskily, much to the other woman's obvious relief. 'Jordan just isn't here.'

'He hasn't left, has he?' she groaned. 'I haven't driven all this way for nothing?'

'Oh, no, he's still here. At least, he's still staying here,' Grace confirmed stiltedly. 'He just isn't here at the moment. He—he's taken my brother to the cinema,' she explained lamely.

Timothy had been far too tired to go to school this morning, and so, after going in to see Jessie in hospital earlier, Jordan had offered to take Timothy out for tea and then on to the early showing of a film that was all the rage with the youngsters at the moment, and which Grace hadn't yet found the time to take him to. As it was Saturday tomorrow, she wasn't too worried if he was a little later to bed tonight, and to be completely honest she had been glad to have him diverted in this way, still being deeply worried about the consequences of Peter Amery, who hadn't yet found the decency to go to see his mother, let alone come here to cause trouble!

The woman standing in front of her looked a little taken aback at this information. 'Jordan has gone to the cinema . . .?' If Grace had said he had taken a trip to the moon the woman couldn't have looked more astounded!

'Yes, he—— Look, you had better come in,' Grace invited awkwardly; they really couldn't continue this conversation standing on the doorstep—for one thing there was still snow on the ground, and it was freezing cold outside! Besides, Jordan wouldn't be back for at least another hour or so yet.

'I would love to,' the woman grinned gratefully. 'I'll just go and get the baby from the car.'

Baby? Baby! My God, Jordan wasn't just married, he—— Baby...?

The woman grimaced. 'She fell asleep in the back of the car ages ago, so I'll probably have her awake most of the evening now. I won't be a minute.' She turned and hurried off.

She... Suddenly Grace knew exactly who this woman was. A little belatedly she went over to the car to help carry the baby-bag that had appeared on the snow-covered gravel, while the woman bent inside the back of the car to unlock the baby's car seat.

Grace looked at her with new eyes, seeing the firmness of the jaw, the dark blue eyes. Admittedly there was little else to tell of her real identity, but even so Grace felt more than a little foolish for her earlier assumption.

As the woman straightened with the baby in her arms Grace couldn't help smiling at the impishly lovely face surrounded by curls as red as her mother's—as red as Grace's own. Jordan seemed to have a weakness for redheads!

'This must be Diana,' she murmured admiringly, touching one starfish hand, finding herself the focus of dark grey eyes. 'And you're Rhea,

Jordan's sister,' she said more confidently. 'You must have thought me very rude just now,' she apologised ruefully as they walked over to the house, the light and warmth inside looking very welcoming.

The other woman looked at her with new eyes. 'Jordan told you about us?'

'He—mentioned you,' Grace nodded truthfully.

Rhea was still looking at her with curiosity, although the baby's attention had now wandered to her new surroundings. 'I hope you don't think me awfully rude,' she finally said regretfully, 'but I'm afraid he's told us absolutely nothing about you!'

She couldn't help but laugh at the other woman's candour. 'There's no reason why he should have done,' she dismissed lightly. 'I'm Grace Brown.' She transferred the baby-bag to her other arm, holding out her hand in greeting.

For a moment Rhea looked even more stunned than she had when Grace had told her of Jordan's whereabouts, but she recovered quickly, returning the gesture warmly. 'Perhaps I understand Jordan's omission now,' she said enigmatically.

'Sorry?' Grace frowned her puzzlement.

'It isn't important.' Jordan's sister shook her head, her attention returning to the baby in her arms as Diana struggled to be put down. 'Do you mind?'

'Not in the least,' Grace invited instantly, enchanted with the little girl as she began to toddle about curiously.

And so it was that when Jordan and Timothy returned to the house a short time later they found Grace and Rhea chatting comfortably in the sitting-room, Diana playing happily at their feet with some old toys of Timothy's that Grace had managed to find hidden away in a cupboard.

Jordan looked totally stunned at seeing the three of them together!

The three most important females in his life were all redheads!

It had never occurred to him before, probably because for a lot of the time he had known Grace he had been fighting the feelings he had for her, but, as he looked at Grace and Rhea sitting together so naturally, baby Diana playing at their feet, he knew that these three females possessed most of his heart.

He was shaken by the realisation, too confused to speak.

Rhea, misunderstanding his silence as anger with her for being here at all, jumped to her feet to come over and hug him warmly. 'I decided to bring those papers you wanted myself,' she explained brightly.

'So I see,' he returned drily, his gaze mocking in its rebuke.

She met that gaze for several seconds, and then she couldn't sustain it any longer, so turned away. 'Look, Diana.' She bent to scoop the baby up into her arms. 'Look who's here,' she encouraged softly as the little girl looked slightly rebellious at being interrupted with her new toys.

Eyes as dark a grey as her father's were turned on Jordan, and he felt his heart melt—Diana was Rhea's ultimate weapon when she thought she might be in danger of seriously incurring his displeasure; she knew he couldn't resist the darling in her arms.

'Uncjordan!' Diana recognised him instantly—she should do, really; there had hardly been a day in her young life when she hadn't seen him—if only for a short time!—and she held out her arms to be taken for their usual cuddle.

The way she had of making 'Uncjordan' one word was endearing in itself, and, after handing Grace the mail Timothy had got out of the box at the end of the driveway, Jordan gently gathered the baby into his arms, nuzzling softly against her throat until she gave a delighted chuckle.

'I was just asking Grace if I might use the telephone to call Raff,' Rhea announced briskly—as if daring Jordan to challenge her.

Grace put the letters and cards away in the pocket of the pinafore dress she wore over a pale green jumper. 'Of course you can,' she said instantly. 'I'll just show you where the telephone is.'

'I take it you don't intend driving back to Hampshire this evening?' Jordan softly taunted his sister before she could leave the room.

Rhea gave him a reproving look. 'Grace has kindly offered us a room here for the night, and as I brought Diana's travel-cot with me it works out perfectly.'

'How clever of you,' he drawled, not fooled by his sister's innocent expression for a moment, knowing she was here because she was curious about his sudden need to spend time alone.

She gave him a bright, unconcerned smile, his double meaning not lost on her, but completely unimportant to her way of thinking. 'Yes, wasn't it?'

Jordan was shaking his head ruefully as he sat down with Diana on his knee, Timothy watching him with widely curious eyes.

The two of them had spent an enjoyable time visiting Jessie, who seemed a lot better today, and then going on to the cinema. Neither of them had envisaged their evening ending like this, Jordan felt sure!

'Come and say hello,' he encouraged gently at the little boy's apprehensive look at the tiny human being in Jordan's arms who looked so fragile she might break; babies were obviously out of Timothy's usual experience.

Timothy touched Diana's hand tentatively until she took the initiative, reaching out with one of

her hands and grabbing a handful of his hair.
'Ouch!' he complained.

Jordan chuckled as he easily released the little
boy. 'Not as fragile as she looks, hm?' he teased,
putting Diana back down among the toys, and
watching indulgently as Timothy sat down on the
floor too and began to play with her.

They might have been brother and sister, identical redheads bent over the toys. The children
Jordan might have had, could still have. That
brought him up with a jolt; he had never even
considered having children of his own before, not
as an actual reality, more as a vague idea for the
future.

What did he have to offer any woman? He was
a man who couldn't even claim the name that
rightfully belonged to him!

'She's so tiny, Jordan.' Timothy looked up at
him with the same enchanted look in his eyes that
Jordan knew he had too whenever he was with
the bewitchingly innocent baby.

'You were that size too once, Tim,' Grace
teased as she came back into the room. 'Although you never had those curls!'

'I should hope not,' Timothy replied disgustedly. 'I was a boy!'

Grace looked at Jordan with a conspiratorial
smile that said Timothy was 'still a boy', but
Jordan knew that the smile he gave her in return
lacked warmth; these two were capturing his
heart, and Rhea, for all that she basically meant

well, had just complicated things for him by coming here.

He looked up at his sister as she came back into the room. 'How was Raff?' he drawled.

Her eyes gleamed mischievously. 'Intrigued,' she mocked.

These two weren't going to let him off lightly about the way he had omitted to correct the impression they had all had of Grace Brown's being a much older woman. Heaven help him when he saw Raff again!

'Not pining away for you?' Jordan returned drily.

'Oh, that too,' Rhea dismissed lightly. 'But he would like *you* to give him a call, when you have the time, of course.'

He would just bet the other man would! Since he and Rhea had married, Raff had picked up some of her impish sense of humour.

'When I have the time,' Jordan confirmed with a vague nod of his head. Raff could damn well wait for an explanation; it was enough that he had allowed Rhea to come here to torment him. Although he had to admit that it probably hadn't been a question of allowing his sister to do any-thing; Rhea was a law unto herself. And he had been missing Diana...

'I've told you before, Jordan——' Rhea's gaze was deceptively innocent '—you must make the time for the things you really want to do.'

His mouth tightened at her implication. 'And I've told you——'

'Grace was telling me about poor Mrs Amery before you arrived back,' Rhea cut in with a frown, intent on avoiding an argument if possible. 'How was she when you saw her earlier?'

'She was very smiley, Grace,' Timothy put in excitedly. 'Not at all like I expected her to bc.'

'As I expected her to be,' Grace corrected automatically, looking at Jordan for his opinion on Jessie's condition.

He nodded confirmation. 'The sister of the ward seemed very pleased with her.' He didn't mention that he had arranged a private ward for the elderly lady; he could explain about that when——

'And she has a lovely room, Grace,' Timothy enthused. 'With her own television, and flowers, and everything.'

'Out of the mouths of babes and innocents,' Jordan inwardly winced. He had felt it would be better for Jessie to be in a room on her own, to arrange for her to have the best treatment available.

He had told himself he would have done the same for anyone he cared about, but he also knew that part of the reason he had acted so promptly was because he knew how important Jessie was to Grace.

He couldn't bear to see that look of pain and bewilderment on Grace's face again. He had intended telling her what he had done when he could find a quiet moment to explain. There were a lot of things he needed to explain to her, but that would have done as a start!

Grace was frowning, obviously remembering that Jessie had been on a main ward with other patients when she'd seen her this morning, but Rhea looked at him knowingly; she wasn't easily fooled, this sister of his!

Which was probably another reason why she was so delighted at having caught him out where 'Grace Brown' was concerned!

Grace turned to look at him worriedly. 'She isn't worse, is she?' She forgot all caution in front of Tim in her anxiety.

'Not in the least,' Jordan instantly assured her, cursing himself for not realising she might jump to that conclusion. 'She—ah, I think I hear Nick now,' he said with some relief as he heard the front door slam, the other man having been to see Jessie this evening. 'I'm sure he will confirm that Jessie is doing well.'

'Nick?' Rhea queried in a whisper as Grace hurried out to meet the other man.

'Oh, shut up,' Jordan rasped disgruntedly. 'Isn't it time you put Diana to bed?' he scowled.

His sister grinned, unabashed. 'Are you joking? I'm enjoying myself far too much to risk missing anything!'

'You——'

'She's absolutely lovely, Jordan,' she confided softly. 'I'm not in the least surprised you wanted to stay on here and get to know her better.'

He gave a weary sigh. 'Rhea, it isn't what you think——'

'Isn't it?' she teased indulgently.

'No!' He gave a weary sigh at her knowing look. 'I happen to feel comfortable here——'

'I know,' she nodded.

'And—you do?' he frowned.

'Hm,' Rhea nodded. 'I told you, I think Grace is charming.'

'I wasn't talking about Grace,' Jordan bit out impatiently.

'You aren't trying to tell me you would still be here if she had been the elderly lady you first thought?' Rhea derided knowingly.

'I——'

'Good heavens, who is *he*?' she exclaimed admiringly, gazing over at the doorway.

Jordan didn't need to turn to know who 'he' was; Nick Parrish seemed to have this effect on the female population. But Nick looked slightly subdued for him, and Grace wasn't with him, which alarmed Jordan.

'Grace had to go to her office for something,' Nick excused abruptly. 'She'll be with us in a moment.'

That didn't reassure Jordan at all, but he took the opportunity to introduce Nick and Rhea.

When Grace came back into the room a couple of minutes later she was very pale. Something was very wrong. 'Timothy, why don't you go up and help Rhea to set up Diana's cot?' Jordan suggested lightly.

He sensed Rhea giving him a puzzled frown, but he gave her a barely perceptible shake of his head, still smiling encouragingly at Timothy.

'Yes, why don't you do that, Timothy?' Grace stiltedly joined in the suggestion.

'Sounds good to me.' Rhea bent down and scooped up her daughter, reaching up to kiss Jordan warmly on the cheek. 'Problems?' she murmured worriedly before stepping back.

'I think so,' he confirmed gruffly as he bent down to kiss Diana.

'Come on, Tim,' she turned to briskly instruct. 'I need a strong young man to help me carry up the cot and our overnight bag.'

Tim was still preening at the description when they reached the door.

'The room next to yours, Tim,' Grace told him abruptly.

Jordan could see Grace physically wilt once Rhea had departed with the two children, their light banter audible from the hallway, receding as they went up the stairs.

'What's happened?' he instantly demanded to know, his nerves stretched tautly.

Grace sank down into an armchair, looking as ill as she had the night before.

'Peter Amery was there tonight,' Nick informed him quietly, although his worried gaze was also fixed on Grace. 'In fact, he's on his way here now.'

'For what purpose?' Jordan rasped.

Nick shrugged. 'It's as we thought; he wants Jessie to go into a home once she's well enough.'

And Grace was obviously breaking her heart at the thought of it. As well she might! So much for his empty assurances last night.

'Why on earth would he want to do a thing like that?' Jordan prompted harshly.

The other man sighed. 'Why the hell do you think?'

'I don't——Money?' he realised incredulously. 'But Jessie doesn't have any money—does she?'

'A few thousand,' Nick sighed. 'Some people's greed level isn't very high,' he scorned. 'Jessie was left some money by her husband when he died, and of course it will go to the son eventually, when she dies. But in the meantime——'

'Putting Jessie into a home would give him some control of that money now,' Jordan realised disgustedly.

'Exactly,' the other man confirmed with distaste. 'Peter Amery is one of the dregs of life. We've been battling against his machinations ever since Jessie moved in here.'

Jordan decided to ignore the 'we' and the air of intimacy the claim gave the other man in Grace's life; now was *not* the time to feel jealous and possessive! He shook his head now. 'I don't understand how any man could do something this callous——'

Grace turned to him with dull eyes. 'Don't you?' she prompted harshly.

The accusation in her voice was like a slap in the face; Jordan hadn't believed she could possibly be as cold as this, to anyone. But she was upset, under strain, and everyone acted differently under those conditions...

'Don't you, Jordan?' she challenged again, harder this time. 'Would you mind explaining to me why you had Jessie moved to a private room?'

That sounded like another accusation. But why? What was so wrong with making the elderly lady's stay in hospital more comfortable? Admittedly he should probably have talked it over with Grace first; but he had thought there would be time for that this evening.

But Grace wasn't giving him chance to do that; all the anger she felt towards Peter Amery seeming to be directed at him at the moment. He didn't understand.

Obviously Nick didn't either, looking completely baffled by the whole conversation. 'I don't think we should start arguing among ourselves just now, Grace,' he began. 'We need to show a united front when Amery gets here.'

'We?' she echoed tautly, standing up. 'You make us sound like the Three Musketeers—but

we're far from being that. Aren't we, Jordan?'
she challenged with shining eyes.

He hardly recognised her like this, so angry,
so—so embittered.

'I didn't think that it mattered——' she shook
her head '—that it was unimportant, that when
you were ready you would talk to us. But I realise how wrong I was to trust you.'

A nerve pulsed in his cheek. 'Grace——'

'It won't make any difference, Jordan,' she
warned him harshly. 'Jessie may be ill, and Peter
Amery out to make trouble because of that, but
nothing you do or say will make me change my
mind!'

'Grace, what the hell——?' Nick looked as
stunned as Jordan felt.

She turned to him. 'Of course, you still don't
know, do you?' she sighed. 'But, you see, Nick,
Jordan isn't quite what he seems.'

Jordan felt himself tense, as if for the blow he
knew was about to fall. And when it did it was
just as devastating as he had guessed, from the
change in Grace, that it would be!

'He's Jordan Somerville-Smythe, Nick,' she
revealed flatly.

Nick frowned. 'Not Gregory?'

'No,' Grace confirmed dully. 'Jordan
Somerville-Smythe is the man who had lawyers
enquiring several months ago as to whether or
not I would sell this house to his company. I said
no at the time, as you know, Nick,' she added

with a scathing glance at Jordan. 'But it appears *Mr Somerville-Smythe* wasn't satisfied with my answer,' she said disgustedly.

It was that disgust that told Jordan all was lost for him with Grace. Had Rhea unwittingly said something to give him away? Had he given himself away?

Whatever, Grace knew the truth now, and it was all over for him with her...

CHAPTER NINE

GRACE was trembling from the effort of trying to remain at least halfway calm; she felt totally betrayed. She had trusted this man, even though every instinct had cried out for her not to, and today, tonight, she realised what a fool she had been.

The worst of it was, she knew she was falling in love with him.

'How long have you known?'

Jordan looked as if she had physically hit him, his face pale, his eyes dark.

Grace couldn't have felt any more physically ill inside if she *had* hit him. She swallowed hard. 'I've always known you weren't "Mr Gregory".'

'You have?' He looked totally stunned. 'Then why didn't you say something?' He frowned his confusion at her behaviour.

And maybe it was confusing, but, when he had arrived here, with that lost and bewildered look in his eyes, accepting the name Gregory when Jessie had unwittingly made the mistake, she had believed it was because he needed time alone, where no one would connect 'Mr Gregory' with who he really was. What Jessie, and none of the others, had realised at the time was that Grace already knew *Jason* Gregory wouldn't be coming, that he had telephoned her and cancelled his stay, and that she hadn't the heart to tell any of them because they were having such fun guessing his name. It had seemed harmless enough fun at the time.

When Jordan had turned up the way he had the other man's cancellation had seemed heaven-sent. What Grace hadn't realised was that his reasons for adopting that assumed name so readily were purely mercenary!

'I didn't think there was anything *to* say,' she bit out. 'I had no idea who you really were.'

'Only that he wasn't this man Gregory,' Nick put in incredulously. 'My God, Grace, you could have been harbouring a criminal or something! You——' He broke off as the doorbell rang loudly. 'That will be Amery now,' he scowled. 'What the hell do we do now?'

She looked across the room coldly at Jordan. 'I don't think there's any need for you to stay.'

A nerve pulsed at his jaw. 'You're asking me to leave?'

The house was going to seem very empty once he had gone, although she knew it would have to come to that. Just not yet.

'Only the sitting-room,' she explained dully, the doorbell ringing again, seeming more insistent this time.

'I'll go and answer that,' Nick muttered, but he paused at the door to look back at Jordan.

'But our conversation is far from over,' he warned grimly. 'I want explanations. From both of you.' He looked at Grace pointedly.

He was entitled to feel that way, she knew. She should have at least told him the truth from the first, but, having met Jordan and formed an opinion of him, she had thought—she had thought wrong! Jordan was a businessman first and foremost. She had been a fool to ever believe he could be starting to care for her.

The silence was awful once they were left alone together, but what needed to be said between them couldn't possibly be covered in the short time it would take Nick to let Peter Amery into the house.

And so the silence dragged on.

Jordan was the one who finally moved restlessly. 'Grace, what have I done to make you doubt me in this way?' He took a step towards her, stopping when she would have moved away. 'A name is only that, Grace,' he added persuasively. 'And I'm not even sure what mine is any more——'

'It's Somerville-Smythe,' she told him firmly. 'The same Somerville-Smythe who is a partner in the company that offered me an exorbitant amount of money for this house——'

'You were offered the market value,' he defended, his hands out imploringly. 'There was no subterfuge, Grace, no deceit intended.'

She shook her head, her eyes dull with pain. 'You must want this house very badly to try to use Jessie's accident against us——'

'What?' he gasped disbelievingly. 'Grace, I don't know what you're talking about,' he rasped. 'And I'm not sure you do either!'

She wasn't a hundred per cent sure what was going on herself; she only knew alarm bells had started to ring in her head as soon as she had realised Jordan had moved Jessie to a private room. She had already felt uneasy inside herself—the names Jordan and Raff weren't all that common, and they sounded familiar to her when she heard them together like that.

And so she had gone to her sitting-room a short time ago to check the heading on those letters she had received from Quinlan Leisure all those months ago. Sure enough, the two partners in the company were Jordan Somerville-Smythe and Rafferty Quinlan. She still didn't know quite how Jordan intended to persuade her into selling this house, but she did know that was why he was here now.

'Grace——'

'Here we are.' Nick made a point of an-nouncing his arrival into the room with Peter Amery. 'Come in, Peter,' he invited softly. 'We don't bite,' he added lightly, but there was a warning edge to his voice that the other man would do well to take note of.

Grace knew Peter Amery well, despite the fact that he rarely came to see his mother here; on the few occasions she had met him he had made enough of a personality impact for him not to be easily dismissed from the mind.

Tall and thin, with thinning blond hair, his face was sharp and angular whereas Jessie's was sweet and soft, his eyes a pale blue that made Grace think of cold, heartless seas.

Grace had been wary of him from the first, knew that he had tried to put Jessie into a home straight after her husband died, but that Jessie had resisted and moved in here. Peter Amery had been trying to get her to move out again ever since, even though he could see she was happy here.

'Grace, I think the time has surely come——'

'Just a moment, Peter,' she interrupted quietly, turning pointedly to Jordan.

His gaze clashed with hers, searching, probing. 'I'm not leaving,' he finally bit out.

She stiffened at his arrogance, her hands clenched at her sides, feeling as if her whole world was falling apart at this moment. Why, oh, why, had she trusted this man? She drew in a steadying breath. 'If you won't leave, then I will!' she told him tautly.

Peter Amery gasped his amazement at the statement. 'Now look here, Grace——'

'No, *you* look here, Peter,' she cut in fiercely, more forceful in that moment than she had ever been in her life before. 'Your mother is in hospital, and is likely to be so for some time. Any conversation we have about where she is to go when she is discharged can surely wait. Quite frankly, I find your whole attitude distasteful!' She was breathing hard in her agitation, her eyes glowing deeply grey.

'But—I don't—now look——' Peter Amery floundered about incoherently.

'You heard Grace, Peter,' Nick told him happily. 'And I happen to agree with her,' he added hardly, his eyes glacial.

Grace could feel her control starting to slip, not least because Jordan stood so silently across the room, not saying a word, seemingly having made his point by not leaving as she had wanted him to.

She had to get out of here!

'You can talk about it all you like, Peter,' she snapped. 'With whom you like,' she added pointedly, her head back. 'But at the end of the day it will be Jessie's decision, still, whether she wants to come back here or go elsewhere. She has a home here with us for as long as she wants one, and I intend to make sure she knows that,' Grace told him challengingly before walking out of the room, her head held high.

It was just her luck to find Rhea Quinlan out in the hallway.

'Hey.' Rhea reached out to steady her as the two of them would have collided, the smile fading from her lips as she saw the paleness of Grace's cheeks. 'What's happened?' she prompted in a concerned voice.

Like her brother, Rhea had a way of getting straight to the point of things, and, much as Grace had come to like the other woman, she *was* Jordan's sister, Rafferty Quinlan's wife, and as such her presence here had to be suspect too. A family conspiracy!

'I should ask your brother,' Grace advised flatly, looking around for Timothy.

'He's upstairs talking to Diana while she plays in her cot.' Rhea easily guessed the reason for this extra anxiety. 'I could hear the raised voices upstairs and thought it best to leave the two of them up there.'

'Thank you,' Grace accepted stiffly. 'I'll go and get him to bed now.'

'Grace...?'

She turned briefly, sorry for the puzzled hurt on the other woman's face at her distant behaviour after their earlier friendliness together. But there was little she could do to change that.

'It's late,' she answered abruptly, determinedly not looking at Rhea again before turning away and going up the stairs.

There was a stunned silence after Grace left the sitting-room the way she did; whatever Peter Amery had been expecting from the meeting, it certainly hadn't been to have his opinion dismissed as irrelevant by the virago Grace had become!

Jordan was very aware that it was because of him that Grace had attacked the other man so vehemently. He also knew that, ultimately, she wouldn't thank him for it. And from the way she had left now he knew she wasn't even willing to discuss the discord between the two of them. Maybe she would listen to Rhea; the two women had seemed to like each other.

In the meantime there was Peter Amery to deal with; Jordan had not been fooled for a moment by the other man's stunned silence, knowing from experience that the sort of bully Peter Amery was—the sort who badgered and harassed women—could often be the worst kind, never knowing when to keep their mouth shut.

He was right!

'Well, Nick,' Peter Amery bristled indignantly. 'I really feel that Grace has overstepped the line this time——'

'Do you, indeed?' Nick interrupted softly—too softly, if the other man was astute enough to realise it, although Jordan very much doubted that he would be. 'Personally,' Nick's voice was deceptively smooth now, 'I think we should have told you where to go years ago!'

A ruddy hue suffused Peter Amery's cheeks, and he looked as if he was about to choke on his indignation. 'I—you—I——'

'Quite honestly, we've only continued to give you the time of day because we didn't want to upset Jessie,' Nick told him contemptuously. 'We didn't want her to realise what an obnoxious little creep you really are!'

'How dare you——?'

'I dare because we're her family now,' Nick said, poking the other man in the shoulder. 'We love her. And we'll take care of her. And if you try to take her away from here, by whatever means, you'll have me to deal with.'

Nick was telling the other man exactly what Jordan would have liked to but didn't feel he had the right to do. Even less so after the way Grace had dismissed him. And so he had no choice but to let Nick do all the talking now. The other man was having little trouble in that direction anyway!

'Understood?' Nick challenged the gasping Peter Amery.

The other man glared at him. 'You haven't heard the last of me——'

'Oh, I think we have,' he was told in a dangerously soft voice.

'I am still my mother's next of kin——'

'What you are is a slimy little toad,' Nick ground out. 'Jessie certainly isn't dead, and she is certainly still in control of all her faculties too, so who *you* are really isn't important, to any of us.'

The other man was all bluster now, his gaze shifting from Nick to the silent Jordan and then back again, Jordan's brooding silence seeming to bother him almost as much as anything Nick had said to him, his cheeks going very pale now.

'We'll see,' he challenged weakly, going to the door. 'As Grace pointed out earlier, my mother isn't out of hospital yet!'

'Little bastard!' Nick growled fiercely once the other man had slammed out the front door.

Jordan agreed with the sentiment wholeheartedly, having found Peter Amery totally objectionable. How sweet little Jessie had ever produced such a son was beyond him.

'Now what the hell have you been doing to upset Grace?'

Jordan turned back to Nick. 'You heard—my name isn't Gregory,' he shrugged.

'And?'

He shrugged again. 'And it's Somerville-Smythe.'

'And?' Nick watched him with narrowed eyes.

'How should I know?' Jordan came back exasperatedly, feeling totally impotent about the whole situation. 'She believes I'm trying to trick her into selling the house to me, I suppose,' he acknowledged impatiently.

'And are you?' Nick prompted.

'No!'

Nick frowned. 'Then why does Grace think that you—oh, never mind.' He shook his head. 'I've never seen her quite that upset before,' he said worriedly.

That didn't comfort Jordan in the least!

'Of course she's under a lot of strain, with Jessie's accident, and that damned Amery,' Nick frowned, deep in thought. 'She could just be overreacting to the whole situation. Although I don't understand what you're doing here, of all places, under an assumed identity as well.' He looked at Jordan with narrowed eyes.

'It's a long story,' Jordan sighed.

'One I'll be glad to listen to, when I have more time,' Nick told him warningly. 'Right now I'm more concerned with Grace, and how I can best help her. I've neglected my responsibilities where she's concerned, been so wrapped up in myself for so long I've let her carry everything alone.' It seemed to be something he had just realised, and it troubled him deeply.

All Jordan could think of was that he had been wrong, that there was something between Grace and Nick after all. And after the way she had looked at him earlier, half disgust, half pain, whatever she might have been starting to feel for him had been totally destroyed in those few brief minutes.

He made his excuses to the other man, Nick nodding dismissively, not even seeming to notice Jordan going, lost in his own thoughts. And from the expression of self-loathing on his face they were far from pleasant.

Jordan's eyes widened as he came out into the hallway and saw Rhea sitting on the stairs, her chin resting in her hand. He grimaced at her raised brows. 'You heard?'

'Some of it,' Rhea sighed, straightening. 'But none of what made Grace rush out of the room the way she did.'

Jordan winced. 'You saw her?'

His sister nodded. 'She's gone up to put Timothy to bed. Jordan——'

'Don't ask.' He ran a weary hand over his eyes, feeling utterly defeated.

'But——'

'Could we please get out of this hallway, Rhea?' he cut in tautly. 'Before I make an absolute idiot of myself!' He had never felt more like crying in his life!

James, as a father, had very quickly taught him that it wasn't manly to cry, and as a child he had rarely done so, as a man never. Maybe he had just never cared about anything or anyone before as strongly as he cared about Grace...? The thought of having to leave here, of possibly never seeing her again, was tearing him apart.

But, when it came to it, he would have little choice.

Rhea looked mortified at the pale anguish on his face. 'Let's go up and say goodnight to Diana,' she suggested gently. 'I doubt if she's gone to sleep yet.' She put her arm companionably through the crook of his as they went up the stairs together.

But even Diana, the baby he adored, offered him little comfort that night.

Grace couldn't believe she had acted the way she had, and still trembled at the thought of her cold anger.

And what if she was wrong? What if she had misjudged Jordan's motives after all? She couldn't wipe out the memory of how stunned he had looked by her attack, his utter bewilderment at her accusations. Oh, God, what if she *had* got it wrong?

All she could think of, once she discovered who he really was, was that he had to be deceiving them for a reason. But what if her first belief had been the right one—that he was just a man whose emotions were battered, who needed to rest here until he felt able to face the world again?

Did the fact that he was Jordan *Somerville-Smythe* really change that? She had known from the beginning that his name wasn't really Gregory, so what difference did his real name really make?

It was *Somerville-Smythe*!

It *had* to be more than just coincidence that he had chosen to come here, of all places.

He had made himself so popular with Timothy and Jessie, even Nick had seemed to accept him at last. The thought that he might just have been quietly and steadily undermining the security of their life here, for his own gain, even going as

far as to make love to her until she was utterly
confused by her feelings for him, was an un-
pleasant—as well as humiliating!—and unpal-
atable one, but it was all she had been able to
think of once she had finally put two and two
together and come up with the necessary four.

'Grace...?'

She looked down at Timothy, realising he must
have been watching her for some time as she was
lost in thought. She had put him to bed, talked
to him for a while after reading him a story, and
then fallen silent, making no effort to leave. He
must wonder what was wrong with her!

She gave a rueful smile, standing up to tuck
him in. 'I was miles away.'

He nodded, accepting her excuse, his gaze
flickering towards the door. 'Jordan hasn't been
up to see me tonight,' he finally commented.

She had been right to have her initial worry
that Timothy could become too fond of Jordan,
and yet at the time she had also hoped—oh, God,
how stupidly romantic had been her own hopes!

She had to talk to Jordan, find out once and
for all if she was right about him.

'He's probably busy tonight as his sister has
arrived,' she soothed Timothy. 'After all, he
hasn't seen her for a while.'

'Diana is lovely, isn't she?' Timothy said
sleepily, without a trace of rancour for Jordan's
obvious affection for the baby.

'Lovely,' Grace echoed, sure that Timothy was going to be asleep almost as soon as she left the room. Which was probably as well; if Jordan had decided to leave immediately she didn't want Timothy upset this evening—in the morning would do!

But at least if Jordan had decided to leave she would have the answer to those little niggling doubts.

The sitting-room was empty when she got downstairs and went looking for him—so were Nick's rooms when she had trudged back up to the top of the house, which only left Rhea Quinlan's room to be investigated; the three of them surely hadn't sneaked off without a word?

She knew they hadn't when she could hear the soft murmur of voices from inside the room, and was about to knock on the door when it was suddenly wrenched open and Jordan walked straight into her, the impact knocking the papers out of his hand so that they scattered all over the carpet at their feet.

Jordan just stood and stared at her for several seconds, as if he didn't know what to say, wasn't even sure of her mood after their earlier conversation. Grace couldn't blame him for that; she felt strangely tongue-tied herself.

She loved this man!

She loved him, and she couldn't quite believe he would deliberately deceive her for his own personal gain, had to at least hear that from his own lips if it was true.

'Jordan, I have to talk to you,' she told him shakily, automatically bending down to collect up the scattered papers and put them back into the file that had also fallen. 'I——' She broke off, staring down in horrified fascination at the sheet of paper she held in her hand, the names typed there seeming to leap up off the page.

'Grace, I can explain——'

Her furious glare silenced him, and she picked up several more of the loose typed sheets, only needing a glance at them to know that this file was on Charlton House, and its inhabitants, on the changes that would need to be made to transform it into a leisure complex.

'Correction——' she swallowed hard '—we don't need to talk at all, about anything; *this* says it all!' She thrust the papers into his hands before turning sharply and almost running away from him this time, tears scalding her cheeks.

It was only much later, when Jordan read the file through completely himself, feeling utterly helpless at its damning evidence in Grace's eyes, that he finally discovered exactly what Nick meant in her life...

CHAPTER TEN

HER uncle.

Nick Parrish was the brother of Grace's dead mother.

It was a simple enough explanation for the other man's presence here, for his slightly possessive air when it came to Grace and Timothy, but it was quite honestly one Jordan would never have thought of if it hadn't been written down in black and white in front of him. In the file that had damned him forever in Grace's eyes.

He had stayed in Rhea's room after Diana had fallen asleep because he had needed to talk to someone who at least understood him, to try to explain to her exactly how he felt about Grace, to try to explain too why he had taken the opportunity, when it was presented to him, to be someone other than himself for a while—that he needed time to find out which was the real him!

And Rhea had understood, although she didn't accept that it was all over between himself and Grace; after all, she argued, hadn't she practised a similar deceit on Raff two years ago? And although he had been upset initially, look at the two of them now!

He lay back against his pillows now as sleep still eluded him—Grace hadn't returned like the virago she had been earlier to insist that he pack his bags and leave immediately, and until she did he was staying put. But he was sure that he and Grace couldn't have the same happy ending Rhea and Raff had found. Some things just couldn't be forgiven, and Grace now believed he had been plotting and planning to coerce her into selling Charlton House to him if it couldn't be achieved any other way; he was sure that was what she thought, and why she had reacted the way she had.

'Go and tell her the truth,' Rhea had urged after Grace had left them so abruptly.

What was the truth? That he loved her? Oh, he did. That he wanted her? More than anything else in this world. That he wanted to marry her? He ached to make her his wife, to know she would be with him always.

And she wasn't going to believe any of that, believing what *she* did about him, would probably think it was just another ploy to get his hands on this house.

Oh, God, he had never felt so utterly *helpless*!

'Grace?'

She looked curiously at the man standing on the doorstep.

Tall and dark, with assessing grey eyes, he was one of the most handsome men Grace had ever seen. But she had never seen him before; she would have remembered him if she had. He wasn't the sort of man one could easily forget!

He wore denims and a thick corduroy shirt beneath a leather jacket, but it was obvious that he would have been just as comfortable in a business suit seated behind an imposing desk surrounded by an army of secretaries.

The handsome face was so hard it looked as if it might have been carved from granite, his chin firm and square, a certain arrogance of bearing in his eyes, and yet the smile he directed at her was warm enough.

Grace *knew* she had never met him before, and yet he knew her name.

Unless he had come from Peter Amery, she realised with a sinking heart. It would be too much to hope Jessie's son would just give up and leave them all alone. But was only eight-thirty; surely lawyers didn't make house-calls this time of morning, especially on a Saturday?

Well, whoever he was, she couldn't just stand here staring at him for the rest of the morning; otherwise he was going to think Peter Amery was perfectly justified in believing her incapable of caring for his mother!

'I——'

'Darling!' A glowing Rhea came hurtling down the length of the hallway to launch herself into the waiting arms of the man standing on the doorstep. 'Oh, darling, I know it's only been overnight, but I've missed you so much!' she groaned before pressing her lips against his.

Raff Quinlan...

No doubt about it, Rhea wasn't likely to be kissing any other man this passionately!

Grace looked at him objectively—what she could still see of him. The dark hair was like Jordan's, if worn a little longer, and the eyes, she remembered, had been more grey than blue, and his face was just as hard and angled as Jordan's, although their facial characteristics bore little resemblance to each other. However she had no doubt that, if one stood the two tall, dark-haired men next to each other, the family connection could quite easily be made, much more so than between Jordan and Rhea.

How strange Jordan must have felt the first time he looked at this man and knew he was his brother—— She mustn't start feeling sorry for Jordan. Or, indeed, for the man standing before her. As well as being half-brothers, they were business partners, and Raff Quinlan had just as much interest in buying Charlton House as Jordan did!

'I've missed you too, love,' Raff murmured gruffly to his wife. 'But I think we may be embarrassing Grace.' His arm was still around Rhea's shoulders as he looked across at Grace apologetically. 'I hope I can call you Grace?' he added warmly. 'I've heard so much about you I feel I know you already.'

Did all the men in this family have a natural charm? Grace thought crossly, finding herself unable to resist placing her hand in the one he held out to her.

'And I'm Raff,' he introduced unnecessarily. 'Seeing as no one else seems to be interested in explaining who I am.' He looked down at his wife mockingly.

'I had already guessed that,' Grace returned drily.

Dark brows rose. 'You were right about the voice, Rhea,' he told her softly, but not so softly it wasn't intended to be overheard. 'It is sexy!' He chuckled softly as Grace instantly began to blush and Rhea punched him playfully on the arm.

'I'm sorry about this, Grace,' Rhea grimaced as she and Raff moved further into the hallway. 'I've tried to teach him some manners in the last two years, but, as you can see, I haven't been too successful.'

Never mind about that, Grace inwardly protested dazedly. She was starting to feel as if this family had already taken over her home; they were starting to outnumber her own family!

'Where is our darling daughter?' Raff's voice softened indulgently.

'Down in the kitchen.' Rhea shot Grace an apologetic glance. 'Jordan is feeding her her breakfast. I hope you don't mind, Grace.' She turned to put her arm through the crook of

Grace's, making it impossible for Grace to avoid going down to the kitchen with them. 'I didn't know where you were. And Diana was hungry. And then I heard the doorbell ring. And——'

'My love, you're waffling,' her husband derided.

She glared at him. 'You would be waffling too—babbling, in fact!—if you knew the mess Jordan has made of every—— I'm sorry, Grace,' she sighed as she obviously felt the other woman stiffen beside her. 'But, for an intelligent man, Jordan *has* made a mess of everything! I telephoned Raff late last night—I apologise for not asking permission first, but I don't think you were in a mood to see any of us again at the time!—in the hope that he might be able to come up here and help sort some of this out!'

'And you told me it was because you missed me,' Raff teased in a wounded voice.

'It was! I was! But——'

'You've had a wasted journey, Mr Quinlan,' Grace began stiffly.

'I think you had better call me Raff,' he told her gravely.

'*I* think, for our short acquaintance, that Mr Quinlan will do just fine,' she returned tautly.

'You're right,' Raff told his wife with a sigh. 'Jordan has made a mess of things!'

The man in question was seated at the kitchen table, Diana on his knee, as he fed her from the bowl of porridge.

And, judging by the adept way he managed to balance the child on his knee while supporting her with one arm and feeding her with the other hand, it was far from the first time he had done so.

Grace felt a terrible ache in her chest just at the sight of the red-haired baby in his arms. Diana was obviously fast tiring of the porridge, and starting to squirm in Jordan's arms. 'All gone,' she told him hopefully.

'It is not "all gone", young lady,' he returned indulgently. 'And your Mummy will shoot me if I don't——'

'Daddy!' The baby had finally spotted her father as he stood across the room watching them, reaching out her arms for him.

Raff laughed softly, moving forward to sweep his tiny daughter up into his arms. 'I've missed you too, poppet,' he told her gruffly.

It was like looking at a different Raff Quinlan, watching him with his baby, all the hard lines of his face softened, his eyes no longer cold but a warm grey.

'Raff...?' Jordan stood up slowly as he took in the other man's unexpected presence here, frowning darkly, before turning accusing eyes on Rhea.

'It seemed like the best thing to do,' she shrugged awkwardly.

Jordan's mouth twisted. 'Your belief that Raff can right all the wrongs of the world is very touching, Rhea,' he derided hardly, 'but it hardly applies in this situation.' He looked briefly at Grace as she stood so stiffly across the room.

She straightened. 'I think I'll go up and——'

'Oh, don't leave, Grace,' Raff Quinlan requested warmly. 'The sooner this situation is sorted out, the better it will be for everyone.'

'Raff——'

'Jordan,' he returned drily, his gaze steady on the other man. 'I seem to remember another situation very like this one two years ago.'

Jordan sighed. 'This is hardly likely to have the same outcome.'

The other man shrugged. 'That all depends on whether or not you want it to.'

Dark blue eyes flashed with anger. 'Don't be so damned stupid!'

'Right,' Raff grinned, satisfied with the answer, aggressively as it had been given. 'I've brought a contract with me, Grace—one I think you should see before——'

'I've already told Jordan, and now I'll tell you, I'm not interested in anything you have to offer me,' Grace cut in furiously. How dared they come into her home and try to do this to her? How *dared* they?

'I think you'll be interested in this,' Raff drawled unabashedly.

'Raff, what the hell do you think you're doing?' Jordan looked dazedly at the other man. 'You aren't helping at all!'

'But I will,' the other man assured him confidently. 'I will.' He put Diana into her mother's waiting arms, and reached into the breast pocket of his leather jacket to pull out a single sheet of paper, slowly unfolding it before handing it to Jordan. 'Read that, brother mine, before you accuse me of making matters worse,' he drawled, turning to Grace as Jordan began to frown over the single sheet of paper. 'Rhea tells me you know of our complicated family history?' he prompted conversationally.

Grace knew he was trying to put her at her ease, but her attention was all on Jordan as he slowly read the contract in his hand. 'Yes,' she confirmed vaguely.

'Jordan wondered for a while if he should be called Uncle-Uncle Jordan,' Raff continued drily. 'But——what do you think?' He turned interestedly to Jordan as he finally looked up at them.

Jordan shook his head. 'I think I should have thought of it!' he said self-disgustedly.

'Too close to it, old son,' Raff sympathised. 'You'll see I've already signed it.' He took a pen from his breast pocket too now, holding it out to Jordan.

Jordan took it, putting his own signature to the contract.

Grace watched the exchange with puzzled eyes, her heart leaping with dismay when Jordan handed the sheet of paper to her; hadn't he hurt her enough already? She read the contract. And then read it again.

Because she just couldn't believe what was written there.

'I love you, Grace,' Jordan told her quietly. 'I want to marry you.'

As she looked up at him the tears began to fall.

'I think it's time we left them to it, darling,' Raff told Rhea softly. 'Jordan at least left me to propose to you in private; we should do the same for him and Grace.'

Grace was hardly aware of the other couple leaving and taking the baby with them. The contract she held in her hand, signed by both partners of Quinlan Leisure, stated that the said company had no intention now, or in the future, of making any attempt to purchase Charlton House from its owner Grace Brown!

It had to be the most reverse contract ever written, and yet it released the chains that had been strangling her heart ever since she had realised who Jordan really was.

'Did you mean it?' her voice was huskily soft.

'Of course I mean it, Grace; the contract is binding——'

'Not that bit.' She let the contract flutter to the floor, no longer important. 'The part about loving me and wanting to marry me.'

'Oh, God, yes,' he groaned. 'It's what I want— would like, more than anything else in the world!'

He looked as if the admission filled him with elation, that aching emptiness in his eyes a thing of the past.

Grace laughed softly, a slight catch in her throat. 'Being humble doesn't suit you, my love.' She caressed the hardness of his cheek.

He swallowed hard. '"Your love,"' he repeated. 'Am I?'

'Oh, yes.' Grace's eyes glowed. 'From the very beginning, I think. That was probably how I was so easily able to convince myself that it didn't matter that you weren't Mr Gregory, that whoever you were you weren't out to hurt anyone, that you were in pain yourself.'

Jordan shook his head. 'I still don't know what made me even start that subterfuge.'

'Don't you?' she smiled gently.

'Maybe I do,' he accepted ruefully. 'Grace, tell me again that you love me.'

'I haven't told you at all yet.' Her smile was a little shaky now. 'But I do love you, Jordan, so very much.'

'Enough to marry me?'

'Oh, yes, more than enough to marry you,' she glowed.

'And to live here with me for the rest of your life?'

Grace frowned at him, not sure what he meant. 'Your business——'

'Goes where I go,' he dismissed easily. 'And I want us to live where you'll be happy.'

She swallowed hard, more moved than he could possibly realise; Jordan was willing to change his whole life for her. What could she offer him in return?

'Grace. Oh, love——' he enfolded her into his arms as he saw the uncertainty in her face '—everything I could possibly want is here; you, Timothy, Jessie, even Nick. My God, Grace——' he gave a self-derisive laugh '—if you knew the bad moments I've had over your *uncle* Nick! I had no idea he was your uncle!' he explained at her questioning look.

'No idea—he——?'

'No one had bothered to explain the relationship!' Jordan complained defensively.

No, probably no one had, Grace realised with the start of a smile. Poor Jordan; goodness knew what he had been thinking of all this time! Oh, dear, it really was quite funny——

'Go on; laugh.' He pretended to be annoyed as her lips twitched uncontrollably. 'I've gone grey worrying about the relationship between the two of you!' He pointed to the few grey hairs he had at his temples, grey that had been there before she even met him.

'Poor darling.' She kissed him there, her eyes dark as she looked up at him. 'Nick is——'

Jordan placed gentle fingertips over her lips. 'You don't owe me any explanations about him. You never did,' he assured her. 'Even if he had been your lover——'

'I've never had a lover,' she told him softly, and watched the blaze of pleasure flare up in his eyes, his gaze suddenly possessive. 'I've never wanted one. Until the night Jessie went into hospital,' she admitted ruefully. 'That night I wanted you very much.' She held his gaze steadily.

He swallowed convulsively. 'I wanted you too, Grace. But I didn't want it to seem as if I was taking advantage of the situation.'

She moistened her lips with the pink tip of her tongue. 'And now?'

'Now I——'

'Ah, here you are!' Nick burst unceremoniously into the room, his face alive in a way Grace couldn't remember seeing for a very long time. 'I've been to see Amery, and it's all settled. He—— ' He broke off, finally seeming to sense that he had interrupted something, his gaze narrowed on the two of them as they stood so close together. 'What's going on?' he asked suspiciously.

'I——'

'Let me, Grace,' Jordan requested softly, his gaze on the other man unwavering, his arm firmly about her shoulders. 'Nick, I would like your permission to marry your niece.'

Grace gasped at his directness, although knowing him as she did she should really have expected little else.

Nick dropped down into one of the kitchen chairs, totally stunned. 'When did this happen?'

He shook his head in confusion. 'The last time I saw the two of you together you couldn't stand the man, Grace.' He frowned.

'That isn't strictly true,' she smiled. 'I still loved him; I was just very upset with him.'

'And now?'

'Now I just love him.' She looked up at Jordan with adoring eyes.

Nick shook his head, obviously still puzzled. 'Does any of this change of heart have something to do with the second Jaguar we now have parked in the driveway?' he asked drily.

'And this.' Grace bent down to pick up the contract and hand it to Nick.

He read it quickly, looking up. 'The second Jaguar belongs to Rhea's husband Raff?'

'He's a little more than that,' Jordan said ruefully. 'But I think you've had enough surprises for one morning. What was that you were saying about Amery?' he prompted interestedly.

'What? Oh,' Nick shrugged. 'Pretty tame stuff after this.' He put the contract down on the table. 'I went to see Amery this morning just to reaffirm what I said to him last night,' Nick frowned. 'I think I made myself pretty clear.'

Grace looked concerned. 'Verbally or physically?'

'Verbally!' He relaxed slightly, starting to smile. 'The man is pretty cowardly when it comes to standing up to another man. And now that you're going to have a husband as well as an uncle for protection I can guarantee neither Jessie nor you will have any more problems with him.'

Grace gave a shaky smile. 'You don't know how good it feels to hear that.'

'There's something else, Grace...' Nick hesitated.

She looked at him sharply, sensing—she didn't quite know what, but something. 'Yes?'

He turned to Jordan. 'You really are getting married?'

Jordan's arm tightened possessively about her shoulders. 'Tomorrow if I could arrange it!'

Nick gave him a mocking look. 'Not too quickly, if you don't mind; I don't want any scandal attached to my niece's wedding.'

'God, how I wish you had made a remark about Grace being your niece days ago,' Jordan groaned. 'I've suffered agonies thinking the two of you were something else completely!'

'Really?' Nick asked interestedly. 'Well, a little suffering is good for the soul,' he taunted.

Jordan gave an easy laugh. 'I might have expected you to come out with a remark like that!'

Grace felt choked with emotion at the growing friendship she sensed between the two men who were so important in her life. Given time she knew the two men would become firm friends. And they were going to have all the time in the world for that, she thought happily.

'What were you going to tell us, Nick?' she prompted softly, having some idea already, sensing a change in him, a change that had been long in coming but which she felt was here now.

He drew in a ragged breath. 'I've decided to go back to London.' The words came out in a rush, as if he was afraid he might change his mind if he didn't say them soon.

'Oh, Nick, that's marvellous!' Grace moved forward to hug him, tears in her eyes. 'I'm glad,' she told him huskily.

'Yes. Well. I'll leave the two of you to continue telling each other how much in love you are,' he teased to cover up his own shaky emotions, kissing Grace on the cheek and shaking Jordan by the hand before leaving.

Grace swallowed convulsively, watching him go. 'I can't tell you how pleased I am,' she choked as she turned back to Jordan. 'Nick is an artist, you know—of course you know,' she grimaced. 'Your file will have told you that. But——'

'Forget that damned file, please, Grace,' Jordan groaned, taking her back into his arms. 'If I had read the damned thing properly in the first place I could have saved myself, and everyone else, a lot of pain!'

'But you do know about Nick?' she prompted softly.

'Yes,' he confirmed simply.

Eighteen months ago Nick had been about to give his first big exhibition in London, and

Grace's father had been travelling to the show with Nick's wife Sue when a van came out of a turning without even looking to see if there was any other traffic on the road. Grace's father had taken evasive action, but it had come too late, and their car had crashed into the side of the van. Sue had been killed instantly, and Grace's father had died a few hours later in hospital.

Nick had withdrawn the exhibition, shut all his work away here at the top of the house, and hadn't picked up a paintbrush since, hating the world, having decided, Grace felt, that it hated him. But Nick's moving back to London had to be a step in the right direction; the rest would come, she was sure it would.

She buried her face against Jordan's chest. 'We're all starting to live again.'

'This is just the beginning, my darling,' he promised. 'For all of us.'

EPILOGUE

IDENTICAL red bobble-hats pulled low over their ears to keep out the cold, blue duffel coats buttoned up to the throat, blue jeans tucked into wellington boots. The snowman they were building was being seriously hampered by the smaller of the two boys knocking it down as fast as the bigger one was building it.

Jordan chuckled softly as he stood at the window inside the house watching them, and kissed Grace lightly on the brow as she joined him.

'Do you think we ought to go out and help them?' she murmured indulgently.

Two years of marriage had deepened her beauty for him. She was his world, everything, more even than their son—the little vandal of the piece outside ruining things for Timothy as the elder boy did his best to build a snowman.

At fifteen months old, Donald Quinlan Somerville-Smythe, named after his paternal grandfather, had his whole family under firm control, was adored by everyone, from his parents, to Jessie, to Timothy, to his aunt Rhea and uncle Raff, to his uncle Nick. Another redhead, Donald had been walking since he was ten months old, and Jordan felt as if he had been running to catch up with him ever since!

'I think they deserve each other,' he grinned. 'Timothy had me up at the crack of dawn this morning when he realised it had snowed in the night.'

Grace frowned at the blanket of snow on the ground. 'I do hope Rhea, Raff and the children manage to get here ready for Christmas tomorrow.'

'They'll make it,' Jordan said with certainty, having confidence in his brother. 'Diana and baby Thomas will nag him into it!' he added with relish.

Grace smiled, giving him a sideways glance as she sobered. 'Nick telephoned a few minutes ago.'

He raised dark brows, sensing something was troubling her. 'Don't tell me he can't make it?' He knew how important this Christmas with them all together was to Grace, Nick having made his excuses the year before.

'He's bringing someone with him,' she said, chewing on her bottom lip. 'He wouldn't tell me much about her, except her name is Dani, and she's helping him get ready for this exhibition he has planned for the summer.'

Jordan chuckled softly at her concerned frown. 'Grace, Nick's forty years old; it's time he met someone.'

'Oh, I do so hope he has,' she said worriedly. 'Jordan, I really do think we should go outside and help them!' She made a dash for the door. 'I'm coming, Donald!' she called as she ran.

Jordan turned to watch out of the window as Grace pulled their son from his face-first dive into the snow, the boy looking most disgruntled at the indignity of it all as he was brushed down by a giggling Timothy.

His family.

His Grace.

His saving Grace.